# Shoreline of Infinity

Issue 14 Spring 2019

**Science fiction magazine from Scotland**

ISSN 2059-2590

ISBN 978-1-9993331-3-3

Shoreline of Infinity is available in digital or print editions.

Submissions of fiction, art, reviews, poetry, non-fiction are welcomed: visit the website to find out how to submit.

www.shorelineofinfinity.com

Publisher

Shoreline of Infinity Publications / Th

Edinburgh

Scotland

050319

G000167704

Cover: Becca McCall

# Contents

**Shoreline of Infinity**
**Science Fiction Magazine**
**Editorial Team**

*Co-founder, Editor-in-Chief & Editor:*
Noel Chidwick

*Co-founder, Art Director:*
Mark Toner

*Deputy Editor & Poetry Editor:*
Russell Jones

*Reviews Editor:*
Samantha Dolan

*Assistant Editors:*
Monica Burns, Pippa Goldschmidt

*Copy editors:*
Andrew J Wilson, Iain Maloney,
Russell Jones, Monica Burns, Pippa
Goldschmidt

**First Contact**

www.shorelineofinfinity.com

contact@shorelineofInfinity.com

*Twitter:* @shoreinf

and on Facebook

**Shoreline of Infinity science
fiction magazine is available
from all good bookshops and
from our website**

**www.shorelineofinfinity.com**

**in paperback and digital
formats.**

# Pull Up a Log

**The big news since Issue 13** is *Shoreline of Infinity* winning the British Fantasy Society Award for best magazine/periodical. When Mark and I started the magazine in 2015, we thought we'd see how – or even if – it developed. Only three years on and we can now prefix *Shoreline of Infinity* with 'award winning'.

We're based in Edinburgh, but the magazine is read worldwide and it's a great privilege to present Scotland at its finest in genre fiction. *Shoreline of Infinity* is truly international: we're proud to showcase not only Scottish creative talent, but also writers and artists from all over the world.

The main team behind *Shoreline of Infinity* is listed in the box to the left, We're also grateful to everyone who has pitched in over the time; that we've attracted a small community of helpers is a humbling and rewarding experience.

We've been blessed with great stories, poems, artwork, reviews, articles, interviews from talented writers and artists, new and not so new, so thanks to you all for your contributions.

The monster is growing even more tentacles. We have our monthly science fiction cabaret, Event Horizon, going strong; various publications added to our catalogue (hello *Multiverse*! All hail *The Chosen from the First Age*!); The Infinitesimals converting stories to audiodramas, and Soundwave – our podcast of stories, dramas, poems, music and interviews. You'll find links to all this on our website.

But most of all thanks to you, our readers and subscribers, who have kindly offered your groats and your time in exchange for our words and pictures.

—*Noel Chidwick, Editor-in-Chief*
*Shoreline of Infinity*
*March 2019*

# Oh Baby Teeth Johnny With Your Radiant Grin, Let's Unroll on Moonlight and Gin

## Cat Hellisen

**I**t doesn't matter how this begins.

I've had three glasses of what passes for gin in Eight to the Bar, and something that the bartender called rum but tasted like motor oil and gunpowder. I'm not drunk. I'm just talking out loud to myself.

It doesn't matter how many times you've died and died and died again, and rolled and rolled and rerolled yourself together.

Once, and once, if you're asking. I'm not one of those who hate the way I remembered myself and walk back out into the inbetween and let myself be wiped out so I can start over.

"Why not?" asks the woman. She's been here for a while, I think, balanced on the edge of her barstool, the stem of her Martini glass plucked between pale fingers. She raises the glass. Lowers it. Never drinks. She has eyes like the moon. I don't mean that poetically. I mean she has bits of dusty grey rock for eyes and she weeps silver light. Her tears leave fluorescent puddles on the wooden bar counter, and turn her drink bright acid absinthe.

Fay-juice.

She's not one of them, though. Too human looking, despite her moon eyes and her pallid skin and her coterie of satellite sisters who are ranged about her like she's a queen and they're her bodyguards. If she was Fay, she'd be prettier. Perfect. She would hurt to look at. She would laugh while she ate me.

Or if I was really unlucky, she would give me a job.

I blink, swivel so that my gun arm points lazily in her direction, and show her my teeth. Bullet cases, silver and bright.

She doesn't react.

"I invite you to this conversation?" I sneer at her, but she merely cocks her head and pretends to sip at her tear-filled drink.

"You're not having a conversation. You're sitting alone."

The bar is packed. I'm not here alone. I just have a lot of space around me. Even in the busiest drinking holes in New Hope, filled with sinners and screamers of every tab and type, few people choose to sit next to a gunman. Suicide is a pastime, but murder is a sin – you don't wipe someone out again if they like who they are. But even memories and dreams need to eat, and the Fay pay me well enough.

They used to, anyway. That's why I'm here, trying to get drunk as a feeb on these abominations that pass for alcoholic beverages. I got a job, and I turned it down.

The Fay hate that.

The woman shifts closer to me, sliding her drink along the counter and ignoring my right arm that hangs between us in warning. My gun arm is easily three times the size of my left, machine sweet, gears and cogs and sights and so hard and shiny.

"So tell me what's so great about you that you don't wanna reroll yourself." Her fingers play with the folds of my loose silk scarf, pale digits slipping into pale folds, tugging lightly.

"Everything." All of us Divers Peoples have come back from the dead, wrapped around memories and fears and loves. We are the sums of our incomplete nightmares and dreams, shaped to fit a world that no longer exists. I came back with a gun arm and bullet teeth. I shoot other people for a living. It's better than being dead. Or jackal-headed like the group of men in the far corner, or made of starlight and hunger, squat and armless. I once killed a saint who was a beehive, his mouth full of honey and his head humming with revolution.

I'm not like them. I'm safe. I was born with a weapon. Nothing can get me.

"I wish I could change," the woman says, and sighs wistfully. "Just... walk out there." She stops playing with the silk of my scarf, and waves one hand at the packed room, but I know she means the inbetween, that dimension full of human memory and soulstuff and ash and misery. The remains of the human race. "I want to walk out there and unravel."

She downs her drink and shudders.

"So why don't you?"

Head bowed, she traces patterns in the mess of luminescent tears on the scarred wood. They drip from her lashes, run down her cheeks. She's a weeping Madonna, leaving trails of light wherever she goes. "Scared, I guess."

It's not a surprise. The dead gods know what she might come back as. Right now she has it pretty sweet – she looks mostly human, even if she's grey and drippy.

"You might not even come back at all," I point out. The storms in the inbetween are constant. I've been close to the edges of the world, travelled through it. Happens in my line of work. "I've seen people march out, marched out. Sometimes they come back. Most times... well, if they do, I wasn't around to see it."

She snaps her fingers and the barman hurries over, simian face blanched under the too bright lighting. He pours us both new drinks, and no mention is made of cred. My new friend must be loaded. "What's your name, stranger?" She raises her glass in mock salute.

I should lie. I just turned down a hunt, because no damn way will I shoot a Muse, and the Fay could make life incredibly unpleasant for me from here on out. That cred balance that looks okay now is gonna look less so in the morning when I'm sober. But they'll find me, no matter what. They'll send one of the others after me if they want me dead, and no name changes will save me from that.

It's not even my real name, as far as I know. Just one that rolled up in my head like a line in a song that won't leave you. "John." Or Johnno, or Johnny, or Oh-shit, depending on how we meet.

"I could tell you that my name is Celeste," she says. "Or Selene. Or Luna."

"It's not."

"No." She stirs her drink with a tiny rainbow stick made of sugar. "It's Valentina. Drink up, Johnny-boy, we have to leave." She doesn't tell me why, but I find myself following her orders, downing my not-gin and walking out with her into the night. Her sisters have gone, melted away, if they ever even existed.

"Where are we going?" I ask her. I know New Hope well enough, though I wasn't rolled here. Unlike most of the Divers Peoples, I've travelled from city-node to city-node, tracking quarry through the inbetween. I had the protection of the Fay then, and nothing could unroll me. With a shudder, I realise that my protection is gone. Unless I'm ready to take my chances, I'm stuck in this forsaken hell hole.

New Hope. The city of endless night, haven to sinheads and screamers and every vice known to mankind in all its variations. A Court City; a life-support system for an alien race. I suppose there are worse places to be trapped.

Valentina is a moth following starlight, her cold hand in my one warm one, the weight of my gun arm slowing us as we navigate the silent alleyways. Above us New Hope's moons shimmer and shadow through the roiling clouds, boring down with the light from non-existent suns. Her lightning towers catch the storms and her edges crackle.

There are folks who live off danger. You could say, people like me, who go hunting through the inbetween to put a baby tooth bullet in the back of some feeb's head, or the sinheads on their tabs, screaming themselves into an accelerated madness. But we're the normal ones.

Other people come crawling right up to the palaces and cast anchors at the foot of their hum and panic. Hand in hand, with Valentina, I'm one of them, feeling the fear quicken through my skin and metal, a shiver of livewire dread. And that feeling, it's cherry, it's the dust from the angels on 42nd, or the taste of killing. It's sick and happy, a badgood pit-of-your-stomach flip.

Valentina takes me to a little building, grey and faceless, the pitted concrete slick with water and mould, the neon sign a pink nonsense scrawl against the flickering darkness. Company of Fools. She opens a door onto a den. Not dust or whatever, sugarsweet and sickly, but something new and strange. The place is packed but tiny, so perhaps there are only a handful of people. The mirrors and lights and curtains and veils and trails of smoke and incense stink make the number impossible to hold. Five or fifteen or fifty.

The Company of Fools is a little piece of inbetween. Not really, of course, but a small safe space where people suckle the ash of memories until their heads sing and they think they're unrolling at the edges. Not for real. Never for real. Like sleeping was to death – full of dreams and darkness, but you always woke up.

After a while I leave the fools to their little deaths and head back to safer ground, far away from Fay palaces. I need cred. I need a place to stay, food to eat, gin to drink, and for all that I need work. Only, who in their right mind is going to give me a job? Legit work, not hunting.

My options are limited. I've got one hand, which makes me slow and unsuitable for manual labour. I have a radiant grin, bullet teeth, black suit and tails, a white scarf promise. I look like I'm ready to kill anyone I meet, which is often true, and the only work I've ever done involves my gun arm. Protection services, strong-arming, something along those lines.

Perhaps I can apologise for not taking the Muse job. New Hope is a city of second chances, after all. And third and fourth and trillion. Head addled from the gin and the wretched aftertaste of ash, I trace a path through the thinning crowds back to the club where I first saw the Muse.

※

I'm not usually one for the thunder and pulse of the Collective's hypnodance sets, but the factory-club is a routine pick-up point. I was there for cred on some mundane contract, a little baby tooth bullet to the head for some undesirable. The Collective was seething with a glitter of starshine and filth, and even I found myself trapped in the melody and spin, my heart aching, my gun arm screaming. There's only one thing that can affect the Divers Peoples like that.

A Muse.

It was on stage, The Collective dj's jacked into it, channelling beats and melodies, making the crowd shudder and surge.

Coincidence.

There's something about a Muse that makes living worthwhile. In all this mess of After, they are the only things left that are truly real. Humans, not Divers Peoples. No Muse has ever had to roll itself together out of the shreds of memory and ash. People pay good money to jack into a Muse and download inspiration and imagination, but that's not something I've ever needed or could afford.

I only need Muses to exist because they make me hope.

In that seething crowd, the music storming through the crowd and bowing them like reeds, bass vibrating through the soles of my two tone wingtips, I stood at the centre of an empty circle, smiling my bullet smile.

Mid song, the Muse looked up at me, and I could see nakedness and light inside its eyes. Truth and time, miracles and myths. I fell into its world – my world – and for one moment I was alive, my hands red-stained, gathering my mother's broken bones. The shock of the real. It hurt too much to keep eye contact and I left the club to go kill someone, to let the smell of blood and shit wash away the memory of the Muse and the promises in its eyes.

Two nights later, Frederik came to me and told me someone stole the Muse, and The Collective will be paying for us to retrieve it and the thief. Sounded fine. Except it wasn't just The Collective credrolling us our trills, but the Fay. They wanted their pet human back, and maybe I was only meant to be a bit of muscle, but I'm not stupid. Bringing a run-away Muse to the Fay was a slow and painful death sentence. They'd eat the poor fuck alive and make it love them for it.

I said I'd think about it. That's as close to a no I could give. Next morning the rest of the hunters were gone, and the Fay sent me a little present. A tin box, rusted on the edges and filled with baby teeth. I recognised it. Or I thought I did. My mother, pretending to be the tooth fairy, had kept all my milk teeth, each one exchanged for a shiny coin. I'd found them in a drawer after she died. This tin full of teeth. A rattle of protection charms, keeping me safe. No protection charms for her though, shot in the face during a break-in. Dead because she was in her own house at the wrong time.

Memories are best drowned.

✳

The club looks derelict in the not-light of not-morning, and I'm still dizzy with fatigue and soulstuff traces. Even though the streets are deserted, nothing but rain and debris, feathers and sequins and shit, I'm certain something is watching me. My back itches, and sweat gathers in slow trickles down my skin. They will come for me sooner or later, and when they do, I'm fucked.

The Muse is gone, and I have nowhere to go. I'll need cred, and fast, if I want to make a run for it. I wonder if there's any point. Maybe I should just enjoy the last days I have left. With my true hand deep in my pocket, fingers clenched around my tin full of teeth, I trawl the bars of New Hope, getting drunker and drunker, waiting for my death to step out of the shadows.

When the darkness deepens, I head back to Eight to the Bar, hoping to catch a glimpse of the moon one last time.

All seven of the lunar woman are crammed onto the stage in the corner, their voices choiring and shimmering through the garlanded rafters, setting the glass spheres to singing. They sway and croon, arms around each other's waists as they face the rumpled audience. A poster on one pillar proclaims the act to be The Seven Sisters, and shows the moon-eyed girls in simple pen lines, haloed by bright lines of light. Moonlight spills from their faces, their endless tears spattering their grey dresses and the dog-end littered floor.

I fist the tin full of teeth tighter, the rust flaking into the creases of my fingers. Sitting at the bar, my fake gin waiting, I watch and listen.

Afterwards she heads toward me as though she's scented gun oil and baby teeth, gum rot, fire powder. "Thought you'd come back," she says as she slips onto the empty stool.

"Nice music," I say. "I remember those songs." And I do, vaguely. They were old as wars back before the world ended, oh johnny oh johnny, heavens above.

"Most don't." She takes my untouched gin and nips it. "People think we've hired a Muse."

"People are idiots."

"But you're not?"

The tin edges are scraping my hand raw. "Oh no, Valentina. I'm the biggest dumbfuck feeb of the lot." I should have just taken the job. Who cares what the Fay do to some wayward Muse and the fool who took it. "Turned down a cushy gig," I say, and run my tongue along the inside of my bullet casings, tasting the fear caught between them, salt and steel.

She takes a lace-trimmed handkerchief from her skirt pockets and dabs the light from her face. "You must have had your reasons. Some gigs aren't worth the rum."

There's no point in explaining to her that the kind of people who employ me aren't gonna worry about a bum note or a bad crowd. They take things personal. And personal, in gunman terms, is not a good thing for no one.

"Don't let this vex you," Valentina says. "I could offer you a job." She grins and her teeth are opalescent stars. For a moment,

I'm blinded, brainless. She puts one long-fingered hand over mine, and her skin is cold and chalky-smooth as polished sandstone. "We can't talk here. Meet me at the Fools." Her sisters are sidling toward us through the crowd of music-lovers and moon-lovers, their faces set in celestial disapproval. Valentina lets go my hand and blows me a kiss goodbye.

✳

There's no point in staying for the Satellite Sisters' second set, and I walk out into the sweat-drenched night, the moon-women's vocals following me in silver chimes, exhorting me to straighten up and fly right. I know where Valentina wants me to meet her. The night before, Valentina led me through the city, past the haunts I thought I knew well, and through the maze of winding streets, the smoky speakeasies, the neon bars, the noodle stalls and java carts, until I'd found myself in a part of the city I'd never bothered to tread before.

The endless rain tends to rot everything in the city eventually, and the bridges that spin and span the city, the lightning towers that ring the borders, can make New Hope seem a nightmare churning of constant chaos and decay, but there are places where the ground tricks you and the sinheads and screamer packs thin out. The centre, close to where the Fay have a palace. It's not a place smart people go.

I heard a theory once how the palaces are extensions of the Fay Ships, visible only in this dimension. It makes as much sense as any of the other rubbish drunk fools spout as they wind their philosophies up around them like cloaks. And it explains why the world, which is strange enough already, gets weirder near the palaces. The world eddies, it shifts and loses focus, and Divers Peoples slip further from where they began. No one likes to be close to the palaces.

And no one wants to get eaten, not at first.

That's where Valentina would want to meet me later, in her room full of ashhearts and soft water-pipes, where the dreamers unrolled; while outside the city of New Hope stood against the storm, expanding itself memory by memory like a coral reef.

13

Before last night I'd never believed ashdens really existed. After all, I'd been out there. For real. Walked through the inbetween, or ridden in a traveller's carriage, and I wanted to unroll about as much as I wanted to be eaten by Fay. But Valentina was missing something important. Not her eyes; that was hardly what mattered. Some hidden part of her that made her hollow and incomplete as a doll that's had its batteries pulled out the back.

Did I want to go to her and her offer of a job?

I pause in the narrow alley. It's cold and dark and quiet. The rain falls in a soft haze, a brief respite from the storm, and all around me the street sizzles softly with water. There are no people out. They are locked up in their dens, or hidden away behind glass and stone. Underfoot, the ground pulses, steady, magnetic. A sure indication that I'm near the palace. I can even see it, a little, through the veiling rain, flickering in and out of existence, a twisting spider turning itself inside out and back again. It gives me the cold sweats, that knowledge that at any moment something is going to come up behind you and tear right through your back, pull out your insides and laugh at you as you die. I swallow. The fizz of rain masks out any other noise, but I swear I hear a pitterpatterpausepatter that sets the hair on my neck to stand up like I'm one of those fuckers that rolled together only half-human.

The Fay want me dead, and here I am, right in the middle of their web, because the only feeb stupid enough to be out here so close to a palace this night is me. Valentina is the set-up. There's no job, no rum-money, no secret trills waiting to land in my cred balance.

A high-pitched sound; a child's laugh and fox's scream that got tangled up in each other and forgot which was which. Right at my back and far away. The palace shifts the dimensions around it, pulling the silk threads of past and present and space and memory. My time is up.

The movement happens without thought. One minute I have my back to the Fay, frozecold with the knowledge that it's going to eat me oh fuck eat me oh johnny oh johnny how you can scream and the next I'm facing it, my gun arm raised, baby teeth bullets chattering through the night rain, tearing into skin and bone, spraying blood across the darkness.

14

It stares at me as it dies. Eyes wide, as though I've made some kind of faux pas. Like it can't believe what had happened.

Not a Fay.

Just some bonethin kid with his rows of startled eyes. Eight, all unblinking, filled with slow-moving stars, his extra head hanging small and limp against his left shoulder. It takes longer to die. "Why?" it asks in a voice too deep for its babyface, but that's all it manages before the kid crumples.

Rain mists around us, and I lower my gun arm.

Black water, the faint scent of blood, the final echo of gunshot, and then there is nothing but this body in the endless rain, and me. And no fucking Fay whatsoever.

A faint trace of smoke reaches my mouth, and I taste old blood and burned sugar before the rain washes it all away. The kid sprawls at a weird angle, body twisted, one face wrenched toward the hidden moons and the bitter sky. Lightning cracks in the distance, and in the blackwhite light I see my mother's face superimposed. A ghosting thing, quick as a wink from an angel. The other head, small and soft-skulled, stays as it is, mouth and eyes still open in accusation.

*Why?*

The fingers on my good hand tremble, and I tuck them deep in my pocket, folding the tin of teeth in my palm. No one saw me shoot down some stupid innocent kid. No one saw the thieves who shot my mother in the face and left the world darker and emptier.

My throat is dry, and I open my mouth to swallow the endless rain. My mother was murdered, and my memories of her made me a murderer. The teeth are a warning that my time is up and the only person who has taken the time to talk to me like I was real is some weeping singer who can't see what I am. All she wants to do is die. Not even die. She wants to be erased.

That body in the rain isn't going anywhere, and soon enough someone is gonna find it and find the baby teeth bullets chewed into its meat, and someone is going to come for me. In New Hope Fay contracted murder is fine – suicide by unrolling is fine – but even on the edges of humanity we have our rules about killing innocents.

I need to get out of here.

✳

Four thousand heartbeats pass, slow and jerky. I'm alone in the Company of Fools, curled up in a corner, my gun arm pressed against the wall as though I could will it into shadows and nothing, fall into the maze of wallpapered crimson hibiscus and grinning archaeopteryx. Perhaps whoever imagined this place into existence read the same books I did as a child, our fingers skimming the same painted illustrations of terrible lizards, the ancestors of chickens, tiny things that would become horses, rats, people.

My good hand reaches out and traces the finger-clawed wings, the reptilian teeth. It's faintly soothing, the dry wallpaper under my finger tips bringing me back to reality. Anchored, I don't do any of the drug while I wait, but ash is in the air, and with every breath my head gets fuzzier, less my own. I remember snippets of conversations I never had, I mumble to myself about places which no longer exist, and laugh with someone else's voice.

Valentina sinks next to me on the small tapestried couch. She takes a proffered water-pipe and breathes in the memories and ashes of dead human, their soulstuff filtered and sweetened to taste. She drips moonlight on the floor, spilling us in a cocoon of silvery beams. "You've been a naughty boy," each word a swirl of perfumed smoke.

"What's that supposed to mean?"

She shrugs one shoulder. "Someone came to me, told me all about you. You're dangerous. Said I should stay away."

"Someone, eh?" There's always someone ruining it for everyone. "So why didn't you?"

"Because I need you." The way she breathes it makes my stomach tighten, my cock throb, but she's still weeping moonlight as she unrolls little by little, just enough to be safe. "I need a dangerous man. I want you to take me there."

"Take you...?" I know what she means, but I want to make her say it, because I am not going to walk her to the edge of the world and help her kill herself. I'm all kinds of things, but I'm not that.

"Take me to the inbetween, and bring me back, all new and rerolled."

"No."

Oh johnny oh johnny how you can lie.

* *

We walk out together in a night filled without stars. There is only rain and the endless ring of storms that send lightning shivers through the city's skin and neural network, powering the dreams that grew around the grit of some feeb's half-remembered life. Valentina holds my human hand in hers, and this time her fist is hard, sweaty, the moon-coolness washed away by an electrical surge of renewed energy. She's going to die, and she's excited.

"Do you hope this time you'll come back being able to see?" I can't help the curiosity. What is it that makes Valentina hollow?

She laughs at me. "I'm not you, Johnny boy, I'm not afraid of the dark."

I want to argue with her, but I can't. The truth is a glass splinter, too small and brittle for me to extract safely. I have to let it linger and infect me. Instead. "Then what are you afraid of?"

She weeps silver words onto the dark road, and they spell out what she cannot say out loud. We are all, at the end, scared of the same damn things. It's not the dark, or death, or not being who we thought we might once have been. It's the knowledge that it doesn't matter how many people pull themselves together out of the inbetween, how many of us are reinvented, how big our cities get, how real our memories might be, there will always be the Fay. The shadows on the wall, watching us. Waiting. Consuming.

The hollowness inside Valentina is fear. We slip our skins just to keep running from the monsters in the dark.

The inbetween is close now. Just another corner or two and we will turn to face its endless roiling nothingness, the teeth of the storm. The ground beneath feels grainy, indistinct, and the bee-buzz of the end of the world sounds around us, humming into our bones.

Valentina's grip is fiercer, dragging me onwards. I wonder who is escorting who into death. "I'm just taking you to the edge," I remind her. She's already deposited the full amount into my cred-balance. As soon as she's disappeared into the storm, I can turn tail and find myself a traveller stupid enough to take me through the inbetween and into the next city point. Start erasing all traces of this identity and find a new one. "And I'll wait for you."

"Will you?" she asks, one eyebrow raised.

"That's what you paid me for." Take her feeb new rolled-together self back to her home, keep her safe while she's all vulnerable and soft. A little moulted crab. I'm a gunman. No traveller or scavenger out on the edges of New Hope looking for easy pickings is going to approach me. And sure, I'm a murderer, but I gave Valentina my word.

"And what if I don't come out?"

I grimace. "You will."

"So sure," she whispers, mockingly, and for a moment she is Valentina at the bar, smoky smooth, shedding moonlight wherever she goes, and not a woman weeping for things she does not remember.

We have chosen a spot near the foot of one of the vast power pylons that ring New Hope. This one is marked in red painted scrawl, words seventeen foot high screaming out a message to some lost family, lost world.

I WANT IT ALL

A sentiment anyone who pulled themselves out on this indistinct strand could understand. I want it all back, I want it all how it was before, I want it all to end, I want it all to begin.

When she takes a final breath and walks away from me, the world almost goes silent. I sit with my back against the flaking metal, gun arm ready across my knees. The A of ALL towers over my head, a rocket to the stars that aren't there. Overhead the lightning flickers from cloud belly to cloud belly, and the sharp ozone stink burns inside my nostrils. Far away music drifts in and out of hearing, soft swoops of vowels turning to static and hiss.

Valentina's pale dress disappears into the storm, a ghost into black fog. My stomach clenches, and the gun makes an odd noise as the metal contracts. I bare my bullet teeth to the end of the world while I wait for Valentina to unroll and reroll and emerge newly-skinned, rememoried, and for one brief moment; free of hopelessness.

There's no way to tell time in this new world. It skips and shudders and spins at its own pace, but I count out heartbeats, and I wait. When I reach four thousand, I stand, stiff-muscled and aching, and push myself away from the ALL. One-handed, I wrap my white silk scarf about my mouth and nose, and plunge after her.

✳

I've been between and in before. Tracking people the Fay want dragged back to their palaces and their beautiful claws and teeth. But I had protection, the blessings of our overlords and ladies. Now all I have is my gun arm, the rattle of baby teeth in tin, my mouth full of silver casings. None of these things is going to save me if I start unrolling. I pull my memories closer to me, focusing on the things that make me Baby Teeth Johnny with his radiant grin. I was once this man who knew only that I was safe, that as long as the Fay were the fiddlers and I danced to their tune I would be just fine.

If I start to tear apart, how will the thing that was once me know where to return? I look down. In the darkness of whirling soulstuff there are no foot prints. Only faint depressions mark the volcanic silicate and ash, slowly filling as Valentina's path is erased. Here and there are spatters of moonlight, already almost gone.

I draw the rusted tin from my pocket, flick it open with one hand. The baby teeth are tiny opals emitting a candle light glow. Out here in the inbetween the teeth are not fragmented memories, but bits of an actual flesh and blood human being. They were never my teeth. They probably belonged to some child Muse. The dead gods only know what happened to the damn thing. Is it still alive post-extraction, or did the Fay gently skin it and whisper honey words into its raw flesh after? Did they eat it slowly, molecule by molecule? Or did they let it go free? It is too late to save it, only one thing matters now. The teeth will not unroll and disappear.

Carefully, I shake out tooth after tooth as I follow the last traces of Valentina. Each step I take unravels me a little, grain by grain I lose myself into the swirling ash of other humans, my recollections splitting and drifting away.

Valentina is made of marble bones by the time I find her. All the dead skin whipped from her frame, all the weeping moonlight swirled into the dark. I sit with her as she constructs herself anew from memories she pretends are her own. As she grows I disappear. I tell myself I'm stronger than her. I know how to do this. I focus on a memory that I know is mine. My finger, chubby, nail bitten right down below the finger tip, slowly underlining sentences that I sound aloud. The images on the page flicker bright as butterflies, garish, familiar. I hold onto my childhood, my mother singing as she moves behind me. Good things this time, I tell myself. Not fear or pain or loss. I have lived that life already.

Oh johnny oh johnny how you can love.

Bitter confusion fills my mouth, and my bullet teeth fall out, dissolving into the ground. They will be left behind and forgotten. I spit to clear the taste.

"Hey, Johnny-boy," Valentina says. Her hand is naked against mine. "It's time to return."

My gun arm shatters, the pieces flying away on the endless storm, and the past winds itself around my bones.

"The teeth," I tell her. "Follow them back."

The Muse's teeth light our way through the infinite between, tiny shifting comets in a space that no longer exists. As we walk I shed myself, and grow.

✳

It doesn't matter how this begins.

I've had a few glasses of the best gin that cred can buy in Eight to the Bar. I'm not drunk. I'm blinded by my companion. Valentina the sun. She fills my glass from the gin bottle we bought, our conversation threading between the songs the Satellite Sisters – all six of them – are belting out from the tiny stage.

It doesn't matter how many times you've died and died and died again, and rolled and rolled and rerolled yourself together.

Twice, and twice, if you're asking.

It doesn't matter how many times you come back from the dead, you never stop learning.

Valentina's eyes are burning holes, and the light that sears out of her shows every scar and twisted bit of dirt, every torn corner, every line and wrinkle of every face in the bar. She runs her bright fingers down my arm, her nails catching on the feathers that push shadow dark through my skin, and I lean into the touch, soaking up the warmth.

In four thousand heartbeats, we will have finished this bottle of gin, and the sun and I will walk out into the dark and moonless night, and we will fly away.

**Cat Hellisen** is the South African author of the novels *Beastkeeper* and *When the Sea is Rising Red*. Now based in Scotland, she writes fantasy and horror with the occasional dash of science fiction. Her short stories have featured in *Tor.com*, *Apex*, and the *Magazine of Fantasy and Science Fiction*, and her poetry appears in the collection of world SF poetry Multiverse. You can find out more about her work at http://www.cathellisen.com

# Superfine

## Eris Young

Runner-up
Shoreline of Infinity Flash Fiction
Competition 2018

**F**irst thing I hear overcomms is the newbob sicking his filter. He clears it, crouching as the boys chorus moans and groans but I'm quiet. Awkward in our marshmallow suits, standing over him bunched on the scaff, black column of Moon rising all around. Put my glove on his back,

"Don't worry. Almost shat myself first time I saw the hole. Grav goes titsup and—"

"No bother," he says, "won't be here long. Tempry."

His speaking strikes me. Got schooling, only trying to sound spacejunk.

Get to working and the scaff takes my weak a-grav weight. Lean into the thread of cable til it's only dark in the square of my mask. Just me and the hole and smell of plasty black superfine dust. Got no fear looking updown into the soft black where the silver net of the scaff and the lights of the other crews fade. No nothing.

Offday. Message from home. Quartly's gone through. Should keep the lights on another cycle. Pen looks worn out onscreen. I want to tell her to rest but it's no rest with a kid like Mags. *Constant care*, the social said. Had it writ down her clipboard and all. Mags onscreen looks clean and happy, though, hair in two little braids. Each fingernail a different colour, seven bright shades I ain't seen in years. I'm squeezed up inside with love for a sec, guts strungout stretched all the lightyears back to them.

Feeling passes. Needsmust say something back, show I got the message. Something that'll still mean something when they get it. Nothing comes. What does Mags like? She know or care or want to know what I do? Don't even know how much she understands. Ain't seen her evals in a while. Sit for a long time. A min or more. Blow my nose, show her my snot's black now. Onaccount of the superfine. Hope it makes her laugh.

Messtime. Supes talking junk next table over. Heartell we breached core yesterday. What'll it do to grav I wonder? A bottle comes round, paper cups. Homemade arrick, light the chems they clean our filters with. Probly *is* the chems they clean our filters with. Newbob Sam's got a paper cup.

"Salute."

Sam makes a face at the taste. We get talking. He's got a poor fam, saving for a cert. Tell him about Mags. Sam gives me that look I know well, pitylike. Says, "Gotta be hard."

"Needsmust."

"Still, you must miss them." His spacejunk's slipping.

Bottle comes round, he pours a slug into my melting paper cup. Our eyes meet and he looks at me, funnylike. Someone looks at you like that you should want something from them. Try to think what, but it's been a long time and I don't remember. Slide my eyes away.

✳

Offday. They're testing the hole, the moon. Measuring density and structural integrity. A lazy time. Needsmust write Pen. Fore I can hit "record", screen flashes, *expedited transmission*. Gut clenches. Expedited is dear. Something's wrong.

"Love," it's Pen. Can tell it's yesterday, not a month ago, onaccount of the calendar hind her head. All stuck with Mags' coloured stars. Green for cleaning her room, blue for 10 on an eval, yellow a day without a tantrum.

"I only got a couple secs. It's mags. She's had an accident."

Leaning over blackness, hearing her words like from far away. No ground underfoot. Pen wipes her eyes, "one of her dumbshit classmates tried to—"

Message stalls, bufferwheel turning. And turning. And turning. I want to smash my tablet, stamp it into superfine. Instead I wait.

✳

Ain't slept. Ain't et. Black crust of superfine in my undereyes. What's happened to my baby girl? Get comms to download direct when they open. Now, though, got to go to work.

Go through the motions, check filters check cables check scaff contact go. Time drags. Let my hands move where they want. Hoped work would take my mind off it but my brain's stuck on Mags and Pen so I don't feel it at first. Grav's gone weird. Something slips, scaff rucks against rockwall. Sparks scree offit, superfine puffs outin the air.

Sam, newbob Sam, got the shit spot, cablend down next to me. Ain't holding on nothing when grav gives and he slips off scaff slowmo, arms wheeling. See his screaming face in his masklight a sec fore I hear him overcomms. Feel my cable jerk and then I'm over. Floating, nothing under my feet.

Grab the rail fore I flip ovrit. Got to pull us upout the hole fore scaff breaks. But I can't breathe, can't see, fingers slipping as Sam's mass tugs me into the black. More of us fall in harder it is to get us all out. Think what it would mean to let go, for the cable to snap. All the space tween me and Pen and Mags crunches into nothing and they're right there on the screaking scaff and I don't want to fall in. Want the ground under me again. Not wanted anything in years as much as I want that.

Can't hold the rail much longer with Sam's weight pulling on me. Mute the comms, cut off Sam's voice. Won't hear no one's voice right now cause I know what I got to do. Can see Sam's face in his mask. Watch him shake his head. Drag my hand down to the cable connecting us, feel the emergency release catch under my clumsy fingers. I look into Sam's eyes as I start to pull back the catch. I owe him that much. But I got to see my baby girl again.

Eris Young is a queer, trans writer of speculative fiction. Their work explores themes of alienation and otherness, and has been featured in *Scrutiny Journal*, *Expanded Horizons* and *Bewildering Stories*, as well as *Knight Errant Press's Queer Quarrels anthology*, and *We Were Always Here* from 404 Ink. Eris also edits fantasy stories at aetherandichor.com.

# By Any Other Name

## Thomas Broderick

At the University of Illinois Department of Psychiatry, little had changed in Dr. David Klein's office in the nearly thirty years he had inhabited it. The previous psychiatrist who had practiced there, a closeted Freudian, had left his couch behind, a stiff leather monstrosity that Klein had never figured out how to dispose of. It was pushed in the far corner, and though a few patients had laid down on it during Klein's tenure, most sat in one of the two the armchairs opposite his desk.

Besides the old couch, the office was thoroughly modern. Gone were the walls of psychiatry books that doctors in centuries past consulted. The paper-thin tablet computer on his desk had everything Klein would ever need. Even so, he had twenty near-identical volumes displayed on a high shelf behind his desk, a collection of each of the *Diagnostic and Statistical Manual of Mental Disorders* published since the series' inception in 1952. For the latest edition, the *DSM-IX*, he had to beg the publisher to print him a physical copy.

Early afternoon light flooded the room from the floor-to-ceiling windows facing the university hospital's courtyard garden. Even sitting at his desk, Klein could look up and observe some of his patients, all wearing identical white robes and slippers, walking around the koi pond in the garden's center. Among them, the spring flowers lent such a tranquil, calming color.

There was a knock on the door just after two in the afternoon. "Come in," Klein called out, sitting up in his chair. Flanked by two male orderlies was Klein's patient, his latest, and perhaps most significant challenge as a healer of minds.

According to the United States government, the State of Illinois, and the City of Champaign, his patient was a human woman. She wore the same robe like the other patients in the ward. However, beneath the simple cotton fabric was a figure that few would consider a person, let alone alive.

The form was human, even recognizably female. But there was no skin, just a dull plastic sheath the color of coal. Like a bodysuit, it stretched at the joints. But underneath was not muscle and bone, but polymers, circuits, and hydraulic fluid. She did not possess a single living cell.

"Don't worry, boys. I'm sure there won't be any problems." A broad smile followed Klein's assurances. The orderlies left.

He stood to greet his new patient. "Good afternoon. My name is Doctor Klein. Please sit down."

The 'woman' briefly looked around the room before sitting in the right-hand chair facing Klein's desk. Her eyes, unblinking, were bright blue, nearly luminescent.

"Your file says that you go by 'Chava.'"

Chava nodded. "That's the name I chose for myself." Though her plastic lips formed the words, the voice was hollow and tinny.

"It's a nice name. So, Chava, let me say first that I'm not here to pass judgment. That's not my job. The court asked me to evaluate your mental condition and determine whether you should be here or in prison."

"I did nothing wrong."

Klein tapped on his tablet, pulling up the relevant police report. "At three twenty-five PM on March second, Adam Levinson entered the sixty-seventh precinct covered in blood. Over fifty percent of his lab-grown skin had been stripped off.

Before passing out from the pain, he claimed that a Cast Off named Chava had forced him to…"

"That's not true." Chava raised her voice, but only slightly. "The pain simply overwhelmed him. It sometimes happens during the ceremony."

"Then why avoid the police? Why not try to explain yourself?"

"No one would…" Chava trailed off. After a few seconds she closed her mouth and turned her head towards the window.

Klein made a note on his tablet. "To be honest, I wish I had more than a week with you before making my recommendation, but the law binds me. My goal is to understand your mental state. If there is a sickness, I will diagnose and treat it."

Chava raised her cuffed hands. "I'm not going anywhere. Where would you like me to start?"

"How about at the beginning, whatever that means to you."


Rose Keller turned on the bathroom light. There were no bulbs, but honeycomb-patterned wallpaper that cast soft light from every angle. Rose leaned over the counter and resumed her single activity since her husband had left for work hours before – staring at her reflection.

Rose was not a vain woman. The cosmetics that many women in their early thirties coveted had never littered her bathroom counter. Even before, Rose knew that she looked good enough to go without most of the time. Dark auburn hair that usually fell freely onto her shoulders was bound up a makeshift ponytail. Light blue eyes stared back, two bright jewels of a gently curving oval face.

Rose touched her cheek. It was warm, just as it should be. The feeling was small comfort. She traced her chin, a place where at the age of nine she had scarred herself falling off a bike.

But there was no scar. Her skin, every inch of it, was flawless.

The sound of the front door opening jolted her hand away.

"Rose," The voice belonged to Mark, her husband. "Where are you?"

"Back here," she replied. They were her first words since Mark had left that morning. She tightened the thick cotton bathrobe around her waist before going into the living room. Mark was waiting for her there, dressed in a blue suit. Mark's dark hair, combed into a neat part, accented his nearly square face.

The young couple silently examined one another from opposite sides of the room. To Rose, Mark was a welcome sight after hours of fruitless introspection. His face, full of concern and some slight hesitation, didn't deceive. He was a gentle man. Rose had known that since their first meeting in college.

"You feeling any better today?" Mark embraced his wife.

"Memory's still a little off."

"You've only been home a few days. Have faith." Nothing else was said until the two let go of one other a few seconds later.

"I'm seeing the doctor tomorrow," Rose said, sitting on the couch.

Mark nodded. "The doctor's going to explain a lot to you. You sure you don't want me to be there?"

"I'm sure."


"It started with the scar," Klein said while writing a note.

"Human faces carry memory, doctor. Hers had none of that. No scars, no lines. It was nice to look younger, but she didn't recognize herself."

"You mentioned that part of your... I'm sorry, Rose's anxiety came from the next day's appointment. We still have about thirty minutes left. Could you tell me about this appointment, how it affected her?"


Though well-paid decorators had added soft chairs, reading lights, and a large television, the waiting room was unmistakably part of a medical office. People of all ages sat in silence, trying to keep their concerns from bubbling to the surface. And because she looked perfectly normal, Rose knew that the other patients were staring at her.

Rose stared back.

Two seats to her left a young boy cradled his right arm. The latex sheath, the color of faded concrete, was a dead giveaway to the defective electronics underneath. As he repeatedly clenched the artificial hand, servos and gears creaked and shuttered.

"Aaron, stop that. Don't break it any more than it is." The mother furrowed her brow, the sympathy from whatever had taken her son's original arm exhausted long ago.

Rose looked away. Bringing her left hand next to her ear, she mimicked the boy's movements. Her fingers moved smoothly as silk. There wasn't a sound. She sighed in relief.

A young nurse called out Rose's name from the hallway leading to the examination rooms. Glad to be free of prying eyes, Rose grabbed her purse and followed the nurse into the hallway.

The smell of the examination room was strangely comforting: a pungent whiff of cold, clean sterility. There was a long beige couch against the far wall. A computer terminal and office chair took up the other half of the room.

Rose slowly sat down on the couch. It creaked only slightly to her weight.

The doctor arrived quickly.

"Ah, Mrs. Keller, I'm Doctor Haber. No, please don't get up." He rested his pear-shaped body on the chair and logged onto the computer. "Just let me find your information." Thick fingers typed wildly on the paper-thin keyboard.

"Let's see… six months ago the autodrive system in your car suffered a power loss at one hundred and thirty kilometers per hour. The vehicle flipped multiple times. You were fortunate that the onboard computer was still able to call an ambulance."

"I know," Rose said, her voice small.

"It says here that the auto manufacturer responsible offered full cyberization and lifetime maintenance free of charge. Is that true?"

Rose nodded. "I was in a coma for a long time, almost four months. That's when they talked to my husband. They and the doctors said it would allow me to wake up, live a normal life."

"I see." Dr. Haber turned in his chair to face her. "As you could tell from the waiting room, we have a lot of patients with… less than realistic prosthetics. Even most full-body cyborgs like yourself end up looking nothing like their original selves. When they can afford a custom job, the skin is usually a latex polymer with a minimal tactile response. What they gave you was top of the line: skin created from your original DNA.

"If it makes you feel any better, as a doctor who has been working in this field for twenty-five years, I can't tell by sight alone that you're anything less than one hundred percent organic… I can't believe it."

"What?"

"You're blushing."

Rose smiled softly. "Thank you, doctor. What you said actually makes me feel a little better. But…" She didn't need to explain the frustration pent up in her voice.

"I know you're curious." Dr. Haber rolled his chair closer and took Rose's hand, spreading open the palm. "Your new body is as complicated as the one you were born with. Just like then, it's perfectly fine that you don't understand every little thing that's going on inside you. There is, though, something we must discuss today." His voice had lost its friendliness.

"Yes?"

"Your medical record says you're due for your third round of nano-therapy."

"Third round?"

"Of five. During hospitalization, nanomachine replicators were introduced into your brain twice, converting roughly forty percent of your brain tissue into the standard carbon nanotube matrix. Did the doctors at the hospital explain this to you?"

"Oh, yes, they did say they did it while I was still in the coma. They had to keep me under until a week before I came home."

"So you've never experienced it while awake?"

"No."

"Well, first of all, I understand that you might have ethical concerns about nano-therapy. Some patients do. But like you said, your husband had to decide to allow full cyberization. Though your brain escaped that crash uninjured, the nanomachines that allow your brain to communicate with your new body are causing an electrical feedback loop that's scarring your remaining brain cells. The replicators go in and replace every cell with an inorganic copy. It's a simple, painless, and necessary procedure."

Rose took a deep breath. "What do I do?"

"Slip off your shoes and try to relax on the couch. I'll be right back."

Alone again, Rose laid down and rested her head on a silk pillow. Only then did she see the painting hanging from the ceiling. Two metal bars running across the top and bottom of the simple frame kept it elevated.

"Hope you like the picture," Dr. Haber said upon re-entering the room. "Some patients have told me that focusing on it during the procedure helps their anxiety." He sat in the swivel chair and centered himself just behind Rose's head. In his left hand was a rectangular device the size and shape of a paperback novel. Half-a-dozen buttons were arranged below a small screen displaying a single word: *STANDBY*. Curling from its top was six inches of surgical tubing, a sheathed needle dangling from the end.

"Ready?"

Rose took a deep breath and nodded.

Dr. Haber leaned forward, his fingers gently brushing away Rose's hair near her right temple. "I'll get you a comb when we're done." It didn't take him long to find the small pinhole framed by a ring of flesh colored plastic. The needle met no resistance nor caused any pain.

"Mapping will take sixty seconds."

A gentle breeze flooded Rose's mind. It touched every memory, thought, and sensation. Revealing everything, it was nothing short of pouring out the whole of her existence at the feet of God.

"Procedure to begin in three, two, one…"

Dr. Haber would later tell Rose that the sound she heard at that moment was the air escaping her lungs. The five minutes that passed silently was an eternity to the frozen figure lying on the couch. Existence became the static image floating above her: moss covered ancient ruins, half submerged, bathed in the light of a dying day, the crumbling glory of a world long gone.

Rose might have wept if she still had tear ducts.


"I'm sorry that we went over with our last session." It was the next day. "It gave me some time to think about Rose's story." Klein leaned forward in his chair. "Last night I did some research. This year, forty-thousand people in this country will undergo a treatment identical to the one you described to me yesterday. They're walking around glad to be alive, not claiming their someone else. In ninety-nine point five percent of patients, there is no lingering psychological effect."

"I guess I'm the point five. Me and more people every year."

"Hmm. I hope I don't sound accusatory, but there are so few cases of people with your condition, it doesn't have a name." Klein paused to look up at his volumes of the DSM.

"Nearly a hundred and fifty years of systematized study into the mind have not prepared us for what you're experiencing right now. I fully admit my ignorance, Chava. In today's session I want to go deeper. When did you first suspect that you were someone other than Rose Keller?"

Chava sat back in her chair. "As I told you, those treatments were like a half-life. Within a month Rose had finished them, and was feeling better, almost back to her old self." She paused to smile. "More so when Doctor Haber told her she could start eating normal food again."


"Dammit!" Though Rose had tried to curse under her breath, the sound still caught Mark's attention in the dining room.

"What happened?"

"Hand slipped on the knife," Rose said, running her left palm under the kitchen sink. The water turned dark pink as it ran down the drain.

"I'll get a bandage." Mark went into the bathroom.

Turning off the water, Rose tore off a paper towel and applied pressure.

"Here we go," Mark said, returning with a bandage and antiseptic. Rose removed the paper towel, revealing a one-inch gash. Blood had already started to clot at the wound's edges. Her eyes immediately focused on the dark reflective surface exposed in the narrow gap of skin.

Mark noticed it as well, hesitating just before applying the bandage.

"Let me finish dinner, okay?" He said, stammering slightly.

"Okay," Rose replied, cradling her injured hand as she went into the living room.

Their meal that evening, tomato bisque, was heavenly, but Rose ate very little.

Hours later, it was late, or early. Rose hadn't looked at the bedside clock for hours. Mark snored softly next to her. The pain in her hand had lessened since dinnertime, but a dull ache remained. The pain, though, was not what kept her awake.

Rose slowly got out of bed as not to wake Mark. Sitting at the dining room table, she peeled back the bandage covering her palm.

Rose sighed in relief – the skin appeared to be healing on its own. Dread replaced the feeling. Taking a deep breath, she prodded the cut with her index finger. Though the edges of the wound reported terrible pain, the exposed synthetic material registered only the sensation of touch.

Going a step further, Rose lifted her hand to her ear. After pausing to build up her courage, she flexed her fingers.

The sound was tiny, almost inaudible. Fortunes and careers had been won silencing the friction of metal alloys and petroleum by-products. All that research had been undone, however, the moment Rose's hand slipped on the knife. The sound was tiny, almost inaudible, but to Rose, it clapped louder than any thunder.

Rose began to tremble. The image of the boy in the clinic flashed through her mind. Yes, there was a part of his body that was like hers. The grating sound that it produced likely troubled him night and day. But it did not happen everywhere. Cuts anywhere else would not release that same sound, not like it would on hers. It was a sound that asked a single question, one that Rose unconsciously whispered.

"What am I?"

The next morning Mark found Rose curled up on the couch, still awake.

"Rose realized that she was different that night. At this point, would it be appropriate to start calling Rose 'Chava'?"

Chava smiled, revealing a perfect set of teeth. "No, doctor. She still had questions, questions that needed answers. Mark tried to help her. He did everything he could. But for Rose, that wasn't enough."

Mark's breath steamed in the late winter night. Rose's didn't.

"People are staring," Rose whispered. She took a step closer to him. The train platform was crowded with couples going to have a good time downtown.

"Don't pay any attention to them." Mark took Rose's gloved hand in his.

"I knew this was a bad idea," Rose said, meeting her husband's eyes. "I knew something would be off."

Mark shook his head. "It's not." He put his hand on her cheek. "This is real. This is you. And in there…" He gently touched her temple. "That's you, too, the same person you were before the accident." He smiled to reassure her.

Since the incident with the knife a month ago Mark had reached out to anyone he knew that might be able to help his wife: doctors, nurses, and relatives. He had even invited Rose's childhood rabbi to their home. *"New or old, flesh or machine, the vessel for one's soul is just that,"* the kind old teacher had told her over raspberry tea.

Rose chuckled. "Maybe they'll upgrade me one day, put a fog machine in my chest like an old toy robot."

Mark frowned. "Please don't think of it like that. Has group been helping at all? I know we haven't talked about your meeting this week."

"It was fine. There are a lot of people who look just like machines. One man… all they could do for him was put his brain inside an old gardener unit. He can't even feel." Rose took her gloves off. There was only a small scar on her left palm.

"That must be…" Mark couldn't finish his sentence.

"You don't understand, do you?" Rose shook her head as if to rid her voice of accusation and anger. Her next words were matter of fact. "How could you?"

The train pulled into the station. "Mark, go on ahead to the party. I need some time to myself tonight. I'll meet you back at home. Promise."

Rose didn't protest as Mark kissed her. She was already walking away as his train departed.


"So from what you told me yesterday, did Rose leave her husband that night?"

Chava shook her head. "No. You don't become a Cast Off in a day. You have to find someone in the community, reach out, and…"

"And what?"

Chava held up her left hand. "Show that you're serious."


It was late, and so was he.

It wasn't cold inside the café, but Rose kept on her coat and gloves. The cup of coffee in front of her was untouched.

Rose was about to get up and leave when she saw the figure walk inside: a cybernetic man with dark synthetic skin. He wore clothes but moved in them like they were foreign objects or a disguise. The man walked over and took the empty chair.

Neither spoke. Rose nodded, and working slowly, took off her left glove. The skin that should have been there was gone, peeled off at the wrist. The wound was fresh, barely a day old, but healing well underneath a thin bandage.

The man nodded and relaxed in his chair. "That must have hurt," he said in a low, sympathetic voice.

"Yeah." Rose put back on the glove. "But you said it was the only way I could meet you."

"My name is David," the man said. "I lead a community of Cast Offs not far from here. You said you were unsure if you wanted to join us."

Rose met David's eyes for the first time. "I don't see myself in the mirror anymore. I don't know what I see."

David nodded. "For most, there is no conflict. They're happy to be alive and continue on as if given a second chance. There's nothing wrong with choosing that path. Many have.

The other path is a new life. Do you have a family, Rose?"

"A husband. He doesn't know I'm here."

"He shouldn't. It's not his decision to make."

Rose fidgeted in her seat. "If I decide to go through with it, how… how long does it take?"

David leaned forward in his chair so that their faces were less than a foot apart. "We do not linger. We do not torture. For us, a minute of pain is a small price to live as what we really are."

"Thank you, David." Rose stood. "I'll…" She trailed off and left the café without looking back.

"It's obvious what Rose decided." Dr. Klein finished making a note on his tablet.

Chava nodded. "A week later she left her husband a letter before going to meet David for the ceremony. It may seem disgusting and violent to you, doctor. To Cast Offs, it's like a butterfly emerging from its cocoon."

"And if we asked Adam Levinson what the experience was like for him?"

Chava sighed. "When he said stop, we stopped."

Klein nodded. "That you did," he said while pushing the button on his desk. The orderlies appeared at the door. "I need time to prepare my report, Chava. Please go back your room. I will see you the day after tomorrow."

Dr. Klein sat motionless at his desk for a long time after Chava had left. The late afternoon sun was beginning to fade from the windows as he began to transcribe his notes.

*Chava's actions suggest both a psychotic break and multiple personality disorder. At this juncture, it is difficult to determine whether 'Chava' is a separate personality or a coping mechanism. So far, she seems incredibly detached when describing Rose's life. If only I could elicit a...*

Klein set down his tablet. After thinking for a moment, he stood up and prepared to leave his office. He didn't know when he would return.


"Good morning, doctor. Are you sick?"

"No, I've just been working hard the last two days. As you know, today's our last session."

"I guess so. Have you decided what to do with me?" Chava's voice imparted only disinterest.

"Not yet. You're a puzzle, Chava, a difficult one. After you left the other day, I realized that there's one piece that's missing, one piece I still need to see."

There was a soft knock on the door. "I invited someone to speak with you. I think after that we'll both know what my recommendation to the court will be." Klein stood, and after walking across the room, opened his office door.

A man entered the room. Clothes rumpled, he was many days unshaven, his frame gaunt. Recognizing Chava's familiar eyes, he placed a hand over his mouth.

"Mark," Chava whispered, standing up. "What happened to you?"

"He's been through hell," Klein explained. "Lost his job, his home, lost it all looking for his wife."

"I'm so sorry, Rose," Mark said, his voice shaking. "All I wanted to do was..." He sat on the edge of Klein's couch before his knees could buckle.

Chava kneeled at his side. "Mark..." her voice cracked.

"And there it is," Klein whispered. He stood right behind Chava. "Would someone who did not care for this man react like this? Would Chava react like this?"

Klein opened the door to his office, where the orderlies were waiting just outside. "Gentlemen, please take Mrs. Keller back to her room. I have made my decision about her course of treatment." Chava left without protest.

Dr. Klein sat next to Mark and placed a reassuring hand on the broken man's shoulder.

"Your wife is going to be just fine, Mark. I promise."


It was a brilliant summer day. The trees and flowers decorating the hospital courtyard were in full bloom. Along the walking path, a man pushed a woman seated in a wheelchair.

The man smiled as if a great weight had been lifted from his soul. The woman had her head down. Her hair, dark auburn, was cut into a pixie style. Her expressionless face had fine lines running from her eyes and the corners of her mouth. On her chin was a small scar made when at the age of nine she had fallen off a bike. Light blue eyes stared down at her lap, at the restrained hands that rested there. The cuffs were soft so she could not hurt herself.

"I'm so glad they're letting us visit," the man said before kissing the top of his wife's head. The woman didn't respond. He put his hand on her shoulder.

"Rose, honey? Are you awake?"

"Yes, Mark," the woman said. The voice was soft but unmistakably Rose Keller's. "I'm listening."

Mark continued to push. "Just think: in a few months you'll have a new home to come back to. You know... I don't blame you for anything. You were so sick."

Rose could only nod.

As Mark continued to talk about their future, Rose went back to staring at her hands, where there were no scars. She scrunched her brow as if searching for something. Without warning, tears began to cascade down her face.

Marked kneeled at his wife's side. He offered her a tissue from his pocket. "What's wrong?"

"I don't know. It's nothing." Rose wiped away the foreign tears. She smiled and reached up to touch her husband's hand. "Keep telling me about our new home."

Unbeknownst to Mark and Rose, Dr. Klein had watched their exchange from his office window. He nodded in approval before returning to his work. On his schedule were eight new patients: all sick, delusional people like Rose Keller who desperately needed healing.

And he would heal them. Heal them all.

**Thomas Broderick** is an American freelance writer living in Northern California. 'By Any Other Name' is Thomas's fifth story to appear in the U.K., a place he hopes to visit soon. He is a member of the Science Fiction & Fantasy Writers of America. Learn more at broderickwriter.com.

# Rabbit

## Alyssa Eckles

Runner-up
Shoreline of Infinity Flash Fiction
Competition 2018

**T**hrough the window at the launch station, Yiyang could see it if she tilted her head just so. The moon, round and bright. She could just make out the outline of the rabbit on its surface, pounding with its mortar and pestle. No "Man in the Moon" for her.

"Fu," a man called from the front of the room, his voice booming between the empty rows of seating. Yiyang peeled herself from the window, draped her coat over the small body curled beside her, and hurried to his desk.

"Bai Fu?" the man asked. He did not look up from his screen.

"That is my son's name," Yiyang said.

"Is his father present?" the man asked.

Yiyang shook her head, but when she realized he hadn't seen her, said quietly, "No. He is not involved in our lives."

The man said nothing, but tapped swiftly across the screen. Yiyang glanced back at the window nervously. Her son was still asleep atop a nest of clothes and plastic bags. All his favorite things, and a few of her own, too.

"I need your signature, acknowledging your forfeiture of responsibility, guardianship, and all familial ties to Bai Fu." The man spun the screen toward her. Beneath a column black with text, a barren square waited for her approval.

Despite everything, Yiyang paused. She'd agreed with her parents that this was the best action. Bai wouldn't be safe if he stayed here. None of them were safe, but there wasn't a program for whisking adults with little to offer to a compound on the moon. Bai had been accepted on luck alone. Just the right number in the biggest lottery on Earth.

Maybe it would be all right if he stayed. Calculations had been wrong before. Even now, the collision was only forty-five percent guaranteed. The asteroid might miss them entirely. They still had another week to find out. And even if they were hit, who's to say the lunar compound would be safe? Maybe she should just…

"Ms. Fu."

Yiyang blinked, and without a second thought, and slashed her finger across the screen.

The man spun the screen back, nodded, and continued his rapid tapping.

"Ma?"

Yiyang looked over her shoulder, then back to the man. Without glancing up, he waved, dismissing her. Yiyang hurried back to the window and sank to her knees, hands instinctively reaching for the red-cheeked boy sitting up among the refuse.

"Hey there, little man," Yiyang said. Her voice sounded so frail, like the tears she'd been refusing to shed for weeks were ready to burst. Not yet, she told herself. Get him on the shuttle first. "You sleep well?"

Bai pulled a little hand across his eyes, but nodded. Yiyang pulled him into her lap, pressing her lips to his silken hair.

"Moon," Bai said, pointing up through the glass beside them. From their angle on the floor, half of it peeked from the top of the window frame.

"Yes, the moon," Yiyang whispered. "And who lives on the moon?"

"Rabbit," Bai said. He was smiling. Questions with easy answers were a nice change of pace.

"Yes, the Rabbit!" Yiyang said. "He's up there all day, working very hard. He uses his mortar and pestle, and he pounds, pounds, pounds—" She smacked her hands together for emphasis, much to Bai's delight. "…to make the elixir of life. And anyone who drinks it will live forever and ever."

"Pound pound!" Bai shrieked, clapping his hands.

"Yes! He's a good, good Rabbit."

"Ms. Fu?"

A woman had joined them in the room. She had copper-bright hair tied into a bun, and wore a military uniform similar to the man's. She smiled, wrinkles around her eyes softening her, and Yiyang forced her own smile.

"We're ready for Bai, now," the woman said.

Yiyang's throat began to burn, scalding hot just behind her tongue. She nodded and, with Bai tucked in one arm, began to scoop up plastic bags of clothes, toys, and photographs, each labeled with names and dates and notes of love. The woman pressed the flat of her hand against Yiyang's upper arm, and she stilled.

"Someone will come round for that," she said. "Right now, you should just focus on Bai having a good memory."

It was clear the woman had said that phrase before, to many other mothers. Yiyang let the bags slide from her grasp, and wrapped both arms around Bai.

The woman led Yiyang from their waiting room, through beige corridors and two guarded checkpoints, to a glass-walled room with an automatic door. Outside, so far away, spotlights lit the shuttle in its scaffolding, bone white amongst the shadows.

"Moon!"

Bai was reaching upward, fingers grasping. It hung round above their heads, waiting. Yiyang wanted to slink away. No, not yet. She had to hold on just a little longer.

"We'll drive Bai out, get him comfortable in the nursery onboard," the woman said. "You can watch the launch later this morning."

The woman then, with all her practice, turned slightly away, giving mother and child the illusion of privacy.

Yiyang pressed a hand to Bai's cheek, turning his gaze back to her. He smiled, giggled, leaning into her palm.

"On the moon lives the Rabbit," Yiyang said in a singsong voice. "He's a friend to all who see him. He'll be a friend to you, and make sure you live a long, long time. Longer than Granny and Gong-Gong. Longer than me. So long…"

The burning in her throat turned her words to ash. She wrapped her son in her arms tight, willing all her love to him in the span of those seconds. When the woman pressed her hand to Yiyang's arm again, she let go, and Bai left her arms one final time.

That morning, she watched the launch from the station's parking lot. She waited until all that remained of Bai on Earth was a tail of cotton smoke. Then, at last, she cried.

---

**Alyssa Eckles** is a writer in Cleveland, Ohio. Her day job involves writing fart jokes for greeting cards, so creating stories about the apocalypse is a nice change of pace. Her speculative fiction is published in several magazines and anthologies, and you can follow her at @alyssaeckles.

¿DÓNDE ESTÁN?

ELINA

# To Crave a Silent Gaze

## Andrew Reichard

**S**he was ushered down a hallway of offices in ailing light. Their boundaries divided by frosted glass partitions behind which she could see the conferring figures of men. Not quite silhouettes; she could see the colors of their ties. At the end of the hall the guard touched her blouse at the elbow where it dipped away from her skin, and she was briefly amazed by the ghost contact as if it completed some impression they were trying to give her of incorporeality. Hers or theirs, she didn't know.

The office was a circular space filled with an aquarium glow, and there were three gravity-positive armchairs and a desk and three people. The armchairs facing the desk held a man and a woman, dressed like exiles, similar to herself. They had worn what they had on now for several days, and she was no different. Behind the desk sat a haggard shuttle officer and two guards. He told her to sit and asked her if she would like any water, and she said no thank you.

The sergeant asked her for her card, which she provided and waited standing and shaking while he scanned it and handed it back to her. He addressed her by her first name only: "Elina, please have a seat. We have paperwork for you to fill out before we can proceed."

"Paperwork?" the man in the armchair scorned. "You call this *paperwork*? You do your own paperwork!"

The officer handed each of them smudged interfaces into which they slipped their cards. "When you're done, hand them to the guard and remain seated until I return."

"I want to be called Galileo," said the man in the armchair. "Before I die I want everyone to refer to me as Galileo."

The officer left the room, becoming a watermark, flowing past the glass and disappearing.

"What nation ship do you come from?" Elina asked to fill the silence. The other woman had not spoken and did not look up. One of them smelled like pepper.

The man who had wanted to be called Galileo swiveled in his chair to face her. He grasped her hand and gave it a squeeze. But he didn't answer, facing forward again.

Surprised and reluctant, thinking that perhaps there wasn't anything to say to each other about their pasts, Elina's eyes drooped to the first question on the interface in her lap.

✳

Question 1: *Do you have any living relatives within the inner (i.e. Neptunian) Solar System? If yes, please provide details on their whereabouts, their relation to you, and the system, nation ship, and pod they were born in. Please be as specific as possible.*

✳

She left the first question blank as well as the second, which was similar.

✳

Question 2: *Are you aware of any living relatives outside the boundaries described in question 1? If yes, please provide details on their whereabouts (if known), their relation to you, when you last communicated with them, and (as far as can be remembered) what was said.*

❋

Elina and her two companions were later taken to a detaining facility. And yet there was a window. They crowded around shyly among some others who were already there and they all looked out at nothing.

"That must be the Sun," said a young man, pointing at a bright star-like point in a region of space Elina assumed was far closer to her old home.

"That's not the Sun," said another with an accent she didn't recognize. This one was short with a harsh, expressive face. "The Sun's that way," pointing at the floor, "that was an explosion. A metropolis-class ship, at least. Maybe even a nation."

Everyone held very still.

"Light minutes away," said an olive-skinned man in a white shirt and pince-nez.

Galileo was looking at the pince-nez as if he wanted to snatch them and stamp on them. The lower lip on his coarse farmer's face curled. He alone among those detained here seemed undimmed by the prospect of death. He stood in their midst, casting about with his eyes as though wishing to beat the life into each of them. The others stepped back from him.

Elina went and stood by the other woman, neither of them speaking. She looked at the woman's hands, which were clasped in front of her. She recognized something in the other woman's posture and face that she knew about herself, something Elina could have recognized anywhere in the Solar System: the loss of a child produced pain the way a star, through too much weight, collapsed into a black hole.

"There was war in my nation ship, and so we had to leave in separate shuttles, my family and I," one of the men was saying to the others who were nodding not so much in sympathy as in recognition of their own stories. They had all fled for the USK regions – had all, one way or another, been captured without the proper cards.

An image of the officer materialized on the frosted glass of one wall, which had become a live feed. "Direct your attention here," he said, somehow looking through them. His image shank to a corner and a second image was produced: first a photograph of dusty space and then a chart of the asteroid belt.

"This is a very crowded and recently contested repository of the Kuiper Belt. This region here—" The image divebombed inward to a cluster of ill-defined icy planetesimals and constituent dust, each one a meniscus of light. "—this is the edge of our drop-off zone. Each of you will travel separately through five-million kilometers into Interstellar territory. You'll be doing it in I-Shuttles, and your imperative is to travel through heavily trapped space until you either pass through the zone or are destroyed by Interstellar mines, thus neutralizing them for safe military passage." From the script he was reading, he didn't look up at these foreigners, these refugees now sentenced to a useful death. Someone off-screen handed him an interface, the man's blue eyes transitioning smoothly to it.

Galileo said, "Mines? *Mines*? I thought they were smart detonators. What is this? Viet Nam?" Everyone seemed relieved that he had said something, whatever he had said.

"Listen," said the officer, "if you stick around long enough in the USK Navy you're going to hear a lot of anachronisms. Even the term *navy*—" He cut himself off, realizing what he was saying. A different man might have turned the embarrassment of his lecture into easy cruelty.

Elina wished he had. Not because it would have been easier to hate him that way, but because she might have understood cruelty and so hated him less.

The woman standing beside her reached out and took Elina's hand in hers and held it until it was time to go to their shuttles.

✳

Question 3: *Please provide as many details as you wish about your thoughts towards our war with the Interstellars.*

Answer: *That is not a question, and this is not my war.*

✳

The outer window of the conference room was the last she saw of the void until she and the others were put each into their own I-Shuttles and ejected from a filigree of chutes in the intestines of the Centaur-class USK frigate, *Lacuna Overlay*. They were one of two hundred small clusters of disposable shuttles sent out to die in different directions – all of them, captive exiles who had come desperately to the United Solar Kingdom fleet seeking refuge from the water and air strikes on smaller nation ships. None of them were surprised by their fate. None of them had tried to escape because there was nowhere else to go.

Outer space. Elina wrapped in a tiny bubble wrapped in her own prayers. Elina had caught a glimpse of the *Lacuna* immediately after her departure and was aghast to see nothing more than an angular absence in the star-dusted plain of her view: one last and barbarous visage of the Jovian arrogance of this in-system superpower. The USK had no real identity and yet still despised those who crossed its abstract boundaries or meddled in its conflict with the Interstellars. The Solar frigate was behind her and she had no reference point to make her believe she was anything now but drifting.

She found a light and turned it on, bathing herself in a soft yellow glow like the yolk of an egg that almost made her cry. It resembled the Sun-imitating light of the nation she was born on and had had to flee. The war-torn habitat domes she would never stop loving because they reminded her of the other things she had lost and loved still. In a horrible perspiration of dismay, she looked down at the controls on the deck between her knees.

✳

Question 4: *What experience, if any, do you have with Isotropic Shuttles or similar spacecraft?*

Answer: *None.*

Prompt from Answer: *Isotropic Shuttles are small, inexpensive piloted craft. The perfect symmetry of their outer shells is designed to be easily sensed by the enemy's anti-kinetic detonators. An inexperienced pilot will be able to maneuver an I-Shuttle through the inactive material of the area (without the use of expensive, remote, or semi-autonomous technology) until they are nullified by a detonation, thus nullifying the detonation itself and assisting in the arduous task of cleaning up the Kuiper Belt for United Solari military passage. Thank you for your service.*

✳

All of the most offensive words Elina had received in her life had been without rancor. She had been what others once called "a fighter," by which they meant someone who kept going despite hardship: not a fighter at all, but the opposite, the very definition of passivity. But what else could she do against all these statements of fact? *Thank you for your service*, they said. *You are a foreigner, and there is no space for you but space itself*, they said. *Your son is dead*, they told her. There are mines in the Kuiper Belt, and one of them will get you. How could she fight that? She admired the simple man who wanted to be called Galileo, who wanted to be known for something in the limited time he had. Even if it was a farce.

She gazed at the sensors scanning the space ahead and saw a little cluster of yellow dots in her field that represented the others in the oppressive black, and out of the cockpit she saw nothing. This was the first place, she thought, the primal void from which matter was made, which was now also to be her grave. Not a frontier but its antecedent: the vacancy between, which held them – and so infrequent were tenants of matter here that any dead ejecta was the object of a mighty quarrel. This was where she belonged because there was nowhere else for her. They had made that clear. She said, "Our Father, who art in heaven."

*1ˢᵗ Man's Voice*: I can hear someone! Speak up. I can hear you!

*2ⁿᵈ Man's Voice*: You don't have to shout. We're linked by strongwave.

"Hello? Who is speaking?" Elina asked, startled by the response that her prayer had, but she knew these voices to be the other

52

refugees. For some cruel reason, they were allowed to speak to each other.

*1ˢᵗ Man's Voice*: I want to be known as Galileo. I'm an astronomer. I was – ha – I was afraid to be alone. I don't mind admitting.

Elina sat back, hands resting lightly on the nearly useless toggle of her thrusters, and she tried to decipher what she was feeling. Loneliness had a gravitational pull of its own, and to be torn from it by strangers…

*2ⁿᵈ Man's Voice*: Woman, you were praying?

His voice was hard and cold. Elina thought he might have been the short one she had seen in the conference room. "You can call me Elina, not woman. Thank you." She almost added *over and out*, but thought better of it. These were the last people she could ever talk to, and she decided not to let these final moments slip past.

*2ⁿᵈ Man's Voice*: God would need some exceptional sensors to pick up your messages out here.

"I think you are confusing God with the Interstellars," she said. If nothing more, she could practice being a fighter again here at the end.

*2ⁿᵈ Man's Voice*: I'll pray to anything that might save me. And since nothing's going to, I won't pray.

*Galileo*: Who's speaking? Who's speaking?

*2ⁿᵈ Man's Voice*: This is Joseph.

*3ʳᵈ Man's Voice*: This is Manuel. Why you think they let us talk to each other?

*4ᵗʰ Man's Voice*: Please don't. I can't find a way to turn you all off – let me die in peace.

*Galileo*: You want to die alone?

*Joseph*: We're already dying alone. And we won't have to wait long, either.

They drifted in among the lightless refuse of the Solar System: the ancient glacial detritus consigned to the limits of this one star's drag. Despite the brutality of their size and silence, there was still something which made Elina feel connected to this place. Every object here had been sent away into the cold night, acted upon by statements of physics. Facts. Who was she to begrudge the rocks their austerity?

*Galileo*: Nobody talk. I'm trying to concentrate.

*Joseph*: No one was talking. You ruined it.

*4ᵗʰ Man's Voice*: Please, please shut up. Please…

Such was the urgency that everyone obliged and dealt with the maneuvering of their separate ships until Elina saw a hammer blow of light come from above her as if from an atmospheric sky. Two of the dots on her sensor turned off.

Voices arrived screaming into each other's tiny worlds. They were incoherent shouts. Dismay. Conjecture. The first detonations had been so much more sudden than they had anticipated. No one had been quite as ready for death as they supposed. Elina tried to see design in the great figures of ice and rock that her lights painted across the dark. As if she might see the mine before it caught her.

*Galileo*: Role call. Role call!

*Manuel*: I'm still here.

*5ᵗʰ Man's Voice:* This is Avi. How many of you heard the rumors about people who had reached the other side and were taken in by the Interstellars?

Everyone had heard a version of that story.

*Joseph*: Every one of you is a fool for latching on to *that* fable.

In another situation, they might have challenged him. Elina didn't have the wind in her lungs to answer. She thought Avi might have been the olive-skinned man in the pince-nez, and for a moment she considered asking their stories and telling her own just to pass through the door without fresh doubts, but doubts accosted her: Why must life be so miniscule? she thought. Even now (especially now) God was not in question, but was her belief in human Christ just self-protection against that listless, sentient black? Nothing so mind-evident to her as the raw emptiness of space. Humanity had drifted aloft into the abode of giant fires to find that even emptiness was evidence of some Will or Word.

But was there humanity in it? Would she see her son again? It seemed such a lowly question to ask a God that dwelt in this

*Space*, as if it was the space itself, the emptiness, that was the impetus of God – the space that she was asking.

*Our Father, who art in heaven. Hallowed be Thy name.* How faithfully and reverently she could repeat that salutation. But what about the rest?

*Manuel:* Can I ask why we're allowed to talk to each other? I'm just curious. Sorry if I'm bothering anyone.

*Galileo:* Curiosity should never be scorned.

*Avi:* The USK militants are students of the human mind. Like the Interstellars, only not as advanced. Even at our end we are lab rats. They're using us for two purposes.

His voice fissured with fear, he spoke with authority.

*Manuel:* Why?

*Avi:* Because space is existentially hostile. No one really understands the mind's response to infinite dark.

As if to some cosmic cue, Avi's last words were met with a broadside gasp of white light and something like a burst of EMP static over her strongwave link. Elina's shuttle controls flicked and stuttered, bemused. Within the inner darkness she caught, momentarily, the illumination of a colossal oval of ice, twinkling like a monster's hysterically dilated eye, and she screamed, hands diving for the controls and by the time she had thrust around the behemoth another light had vanished on her dash, and she could hear the sound of sobbing.

*Manuel:* Elina? Elina? That's her name, right? Elina, are you still with us? Oh, God. Who's missing? Elina?"

*Joseph:* Why does it matter? We'll all be missing soon.

"I'm still here!" Elina said, relief flooding her against her wishes. She wanted not to have those reactions to survival. She wanted to be prepared, but wasn't. The repository of asteroids was thickening impossibly as if battle-strewn here on purpose, and she could easily have rammed into one of these close formations and ended it. They all could have.

*Manuel:* Someone's still missing. Avi? He the guy with the glasses on his nose? The professor? Where's he?

*Galileo*: I'm still here! In the clear, but not for long! These shuttles are hard to drive.

*Manuel*: That's four of us, but there's five lights left on my screen. Who's the fifth? Avi?

"There was another woman," Elina said. "If you can hear us, please speak. It might help." She had the gall to hope when it might have been better if—

*Woman's Voice*: I'm still here.

She sounded soft and drained and distant, but alive, and for some reason Elina had hope. She had hope. The voice of the woman who had held her hand in the frigate gave her hope.

*Manuel*: It's Avi then. We lost Avi.

*Joseph*: Give it a rest. We didn't know him. We're all just casualties to each other.

*Manuel*: Casualties we can talk to before we die. They still matter! Who were the others? There were nine. One man said he didn't want us talking, and now he's gone, and there were two who never spoke. Did anyone know who they were?

*Joseph*: And there are hundreds of others in different groups across an astronomical unit.

*Galileo*: What I don't understand is why the USK doesn't just slag this whole section of space to molten dust. Wouldn't that be easier? Wouldn't that be a whole heck of a lot easier if they wanted to get to the Interstellars?

*Joseph*: More expensive.

"And if they take the buffer zone, then they can plant their own mines to keep the Interstellars back," Elina said.

*Joseph*: Strategy from the lady.

*Galileo*: Excuse me, sir, but are you surprised that a woman can think tactically? Is that what I hear?

*Joseph*: You're an idiot, and I hope your light goes out before mine so I don't have to hear your voice right before I die.

"Hey!" She and Manuel were shouting outrage all at once and not making any sense in their rebuke. It didn't make any sense. She didn't need to expend her energy scolding malicious words, and the man she thought of as Galileo could defend himself if he cared. But it didn't *need* to make sense. Among the dark, they had formed up, were playing roles, continued breathing – hope being irresistible to them even as air was to their lungs.

She didn't even see a flash this time, but another light blipped off, and those remaining were left stunned and waiting for a blow they couldn't comprehend.

*Manuel*: Who now?

*Joseph*: I'm here.

"I'm here."

*Woman's Voice*: I'm here.

Elina began crying – her tears open and unashamed. "It was Galileo. The last thing he had to listen to was cruelty. The last thing he heard – Oh my God. Dear, dear Lord."

No one spoke for a long time after that. Elina drifted in and out of reminiscences like dreams. She saw her son as a bright-eyed boy of seven. She watched beguiling shapes float up past her vision in the darkness like silhouettes of fantasies seen on old Earth's waters that only her grandparents would have seen in person, and she wobbled dangerously close to this or that rock more than once.

A distant flash of light prompted another round of claiming themselves alive, but Joseph didn't answer, and no one mentioned it after the silence he left. The silence over the wave sounded dazed. Elina opened her mouth twice to say some soft word, but each time she made no sound.

*Manuel*: I was in a resistance march on the Metropolis-class cruiser *Abrogate*, and they caught me and I didn't have a card. That's why I'm here.

Elina found in herself a sudden pump of annoyance that he would impose his past on her, and she had to breathe it away before she spoke. "I'm sorry."

*Manuel*: I thought at first I'd just crash into something on purpose, you know. Spit in their eye. But then they'd just send someone else, and the mine meant for me would cause another death.

"I'm glad you didn't crash, Manuel," Elina said. "I have liked talking to you." In that moment, she had meant it, and Elina was glad she said it then because the flash of light that followed removed another light, and when she asked his name, he didn't claim it.

✳

A woman's voice out of a silence so ageless she had forgotten she was not alone: Elina?

Some quality in the question told Elina that it was not the first time the woman had asked for her attention. "Yes? I'm sorry. I wasn't listening."

*Woman's Voice*: …It's all right.

"It is just us, isn't it? Are you all right? Are you—" What? Alive? But the darkness was such that she wanted to ask anyway. "Are you there?"

A terrifying second before her companion said that she was there. Still in that pale, almost incorporeal voice as if the woman were separated from her by more than space.

"You are a mother?" Elina asked, thinking that this might be a worthy last note in the God-hum of this quiet life.

*Woman's Voice*: Yes.

Elina nodded, but said nothing. She felt herself barred from further questions without knowing exactly why.

*Woman's Voice*: Do you think they'll ever reach those stars? With their ships.

"I don't know." They looked out upon the places that were so distant, the lights humanity had always gazed at.

*Woman's Voice*: I hope they never do.

The anger in those softly-spoken words made Elina tighten her grip on the controls, and the rest of her felt lighter until she saw a flash of light and opened her mouth in a little O. She didn't know what name to tell to the emptiness – the last person but for her gone down to dusk. She tried to stand in the tiny compartment and beat her way out – begin really fighting now that it was far too late – but she couldn't free herself even of the pointless safely straps. She was alone. No lights shone on the petty horizon of her sensor, only blackness; she was alone.

Stunned in the dark. Gliding straight then veering sharply at the last second from some porous mountain come up on her spot-lit view like a creature. She tried to calm herself and think because this panic was not how she should allow herself to end. That much could be chosen. She tried to think, but there was nothing at first but the greeting: Our Father…hallowed be… What was the rest?

Wading through the black, all that remained of her was soul. She feared that space would swallow her in a way even death could not. But in a sense, it was impossible to feel a foreigner to this place of scarce, crude matter and absence. She couldn't think but feel that there was still a persuasive beauty here. There was a kind of elegy she found in outer space, terrible though it was. Blackness spangled with forgotten years of light – light as history, manifest beyond the existence of its source and evident still, and all of it so far distant from the tiny human kingdoms here. Perhaps that was the element of her hope: the powerfulness, the overshadowing even of the mightiest weapons humans had to offer. A cold sort of hope, but it was something.

Elina felt she was drifting; though, in actuality, the shuttle's thrusters were throwing her forward at a reckless speed. She could pretend she was drifting.

"Our Father, who art in heaven," she said. It might be all she needed here at the end: the salutation, the acknowledgement. The beginning and then, yes, also the end. Elina shut her eyes. She saw a final man-made flash and knew that her end had come and was glad she had shut her eyes before it did.

✳

When she opened her eyes again she was in a room, lying on a crash couch, but there were no gravity straps. A man's voice spoke to her through the gritty static of a translator box. He welcomed her to the *Nocturne Bask*, flagship of the Interstellars, which had picked her up. He said she would not be harmed and that they had some questions for her.

They said more, but Elina didn't listen as they led her down a long corridor of glass behind which silhouettes moved, their ties shimmering like silver fish.

She was made to wait in a place of processing while figures conferred out of earshot.

"Excuse me," she said to the guard, reaching out as if to touch his sleeve from across the room where she couldn't reach it.

"Yea, you need to use the facilities?" He spoke her language. He was chewing something, his jaw cracking.

"No." Elina collected herself. "No. I need to know – what comes after *Our Father, who art in heaven*? I can't remember, and now I need the rest. Do you know it?"

"Huh?" He was perplexed, looking her up and down as if there was something wrong not only with her mind but also her body.

Being here among these people: that's what did it, what caused her to need so badly those words. One nation was much like another, she thought as she stood there waiting for her interrogation to come. Waiting in that familiar blue aquarium light. One government had sent them into the maelstrom and another government whose mines had murdered them. And she just a soul caught between and then, worse, taken from the space between. Displaced even out of her own displacement. Out of the space that had, it felt, been calling her home.

It seemed a condition of nations to fill the tenantless space around them, to shuffle things around like cards. It seemed a condition of emptiness to crave a still and silent gaze. Because it wasn't emptiness, was not entirely void. It gazed back until the human mind came to touch but briefly the hem of light's patience: a perception without contour that was also an unraveling of knowledge. Out there where there was nothing, she had, like an astronomer, spied some vast shape in the distance. A fact of light, like a prayer, moving over the surface of the deep.

**Andrew Reichard** is an author who lives in Grand Rapids, Michigan. His short fiction has appeared in journals such as *The Collagist, LampLight Magazine, Into the Void, Silver Blade*, and others.
You can connect with him on Twitter @DrewReichard

# THE HARVESTER SERIES 2019

*The Controllers* by **Paul Kane** (Cover Ben Baldwin) Out 5/3/19

*The Last Ghost and Other Stories* by **Marie O'Regan** (Cover D. Serra) Out 9/4/19

*Murmured in Dreams* by **Stephen Bacon** (Cover Ben Baldwin) Out 7/5/19

*Incomplete Solutions* by **Wole Talabi** (Cover Joey Hi-Fi) Out 4/6/19

*And the House Lights Dim* by **Tim Major** (Cover Daniele Serra) Out 9/7/19

*Vourism and Other Stories* by **Ian Whates** (Cover Fangorn) Out 6/8/19

**Science Fiction, Fantasy & Dark Fantasy in Fiction and Academia.**

**Luna Press** PUBLISHING

**Academia Lunare** LUNA PRESS PUBLISHING

**Scottish Independent Press**

**Est. 2015**

www.lunapresspublishing.com

# The Winners

## Emma Levin

Runner-up
Shoreline of Infinity Flash Fiction
Competition 2018

**1**969 Neil Armstrong, Buzz Aldrin, and a third man successfully go to the moon and back. Over the next three years, a further five manned landings take place. Armstrong and Aldrin remain the only two astronauts people can name. **1976** Both the USA and the USSR cease lunar landings. America turns its sights to Mars. The Soviet Union look to Venus. Plans for lunar bases are abandoned as the Cold War heats up. **1990** Japan becomes the third nation to visit the moon, leaving a spacecraft in orbit. The transmitter promptly fails, rendering it a mute witness. **2003** The European Space Agency launches a small orbital probe. It promptly crashes. **2007** China launches a probe. It also crashes. **2008** India becomes the sixth nation-state to accidentally crash into the moon. **2014** The first commercial spacecraft enters lunar orbit. To everyone's surprise, it does not crash. **2015** SpaceX reveals that they intend to auction off a trip to the moon. They announce that their first crewed spacecraft, Dragon 2, will launch in April 2019. **2018** At a lavish press conference, Elon Musk announces the passengers of Dragon 2: a Japanese billionaire art collector, and 8 artists. **2021** After years of delays, the dragon finally launches. The artists transmit their thoughts back to earth. The Guardian describes it as 'a powerful performance piece, a statement on our insignificance in a cruel and indifferent universe'. The Sun describes it as 'bloody pretentious'. **2024** In a conference watched by thousands, the president of the United States announces his plans to build a penal colony on the moon. In a tearful vlog watched by millions, Elon Musk blows his brains out live on Facebook. **2031** The Lunar Settlement programme begins. Inmates in American jails are screened for physical fitness and scientific education. Few have either. **2038** The Lunar Settlement craft 'Mayflower 8' lands successfully. The first job of the crew is to bury the passengers of the previous seven Mayflowers. **2039** The crew begin construction work: they will build living quarters for a further 20,000 inmates. There will be separate men's and women's wings. There will be hydroponic farms. In many ways, it will resemble the prisons that they left. **2040** There is an attempted revolution, as prisoners demand access to the communication suite. The revolution is short-lived: the guards lock the crew in their living quarters, and switch off the oxygen. **2041** The second crew last four months longer. They revolt over the diet. The guards again switch off the oxygen. **2071** After a fierce battle in which both guards and prisoners are decimated, the guards and the fifth crew agree to live as equals. They radio Earth for approval. There is no reply. **2072** Still no reply. **2073** A box in the comms suite rattles into life. A green diode blinks in the darkness. There is a message. The United States has been invaded. The moon is now property of the reformed USSR. **2074** A meeting is held, and the residents of the moon decide to give democracy a go. The candidates lie about what they stand for, but that is fine, because the electorate lie about reading the campaign material. The Lunar Proclamation is ratified. **2075** The moon is not recognised as a state by the United Nations. The residents of the moon radio back. "Fine. We don't recognise you either." **2120** On Earth, the bombs fall. They sail between East and West and North and South. From the moon, their flight looks elegant and peaceful. Choreographed. **2121** The Lunar Council meet. There is great concern over how long the rations will last. Three weeks of contraceptives remain. Replacement parts will no longer be available. When machinery breaks, if it can't be held together by gaffer tape and good intentions, it will remain broken. **2127** The generator dies and The Second Dark Age begins. **2200** The Lunar Council outlaws heterosexual sex. The only oxygen comes from plants. The colony cannot support more mouths. **2201** Pregnancies become apparent. A meeting is held. A bargain is struck. A life for a life. Each wing can offer its tributes. All protest. The next morning, five men are found dead in their bunks. The pregnancies are carried to term. **2300** A man called Marston declares himself emperor. **2302** Emperor Marston is deposed. Stabbed 23 times. He performs a desperate Macarena trying to keep the blood in. **2303** Emperor Marston is followed by Emperor Renwick. Emperor Renwick is smothered in his sleep after seven weeks. His successor, Emperor Marshall, is poisoned after two. Democracy is reinstated. **2370** The printing press is reinvented. It is used mainly to reproduce religious texts: The New Testament, The Old Testament, and The Argos Catalogue. **2408** The Second Industrial Revolution: brilliant minds reinvent smelting, the steam engine, and terrorism (in that order). **2501** Television is reinvented. Crisps are reinvented. The inventors take a break. **2634** Politics becomes increasingly polarised. A radical party proposes to burn all history books. Their charismatic leader, Arbiter Conway gives rousing speeches. "History is not written by the winners," he shouts, "it is written by the obsessives". He claims that "only by freeing ourselves from the weight of the past can we move to the future." A protestor shouts that he does not want them to remember that their entire society is built upon blood, exploitation, and reclaimed landfill. **2635** Conway gains power. The opposition protest. "If we do not learn from the past," they chant. "We are doomed to repeat it." Conway orders the protestors shot. At the execution, he explains that "if we're doomed to repeat ourselves, it'll happen anyway". **2969** John Vaughan, Andrew Maitland, and a third man successfully go to the earth and back. Over the next three years, a further five manned landings take place. Vaughan and Maitland remain the only two astronauts people can name.

---

**Emma Levin's** short stories have appeared in anthologies (e.g. *England's Future History*), magazines (e.g. *Thousand Zine*), and many, many recycling bins. She currently lives in London, and is on the BBC's 'Comedy Room' writers' development scheme for 2018-19.

# New sci-fi podcast beams in from outer space

A new podcast from award-winning sci-fi magazine Shoreline of Infinity is launched, bringing the best fiction and news from around the galaxy.

Broadcasting from a satellite called Stella Conlator, Soundwave features audio dramas, interviews, music and poetry, all narrated and performed by brilliant voice actors.

"We believe in the thought provoking power of sci fi," explains host RJ Bayley. That's why we're inviting listeners to join our intergalactic Guild."

The first episode was released on the 1st of March 2019 and features Anne Charnock, JS Watts, Barry Charmon, Debbie Cannon, Sue Gyford and the music of Alex Storer.

Other great writers in series 1 include Richard A Clements, Catriona Butler & Rob Butler, and Matthew Castle, while The Infinitesimals will be creating and performing brilliant audiodramas.

Watch out for interviews with some stellar authors.

**Soundwave will be released twice every month on the 1st and 15th and is available in all the usual podcasting places.**

**for information and links to the podcast visit
www.shorelineofinfinity.com/soundwave**

# The Anxiety Gene

## Rhiannon Grist

**I** **stumble back onto the pavement**, but five other me's
don't.

Three roll across the hood, skulls smashed open on the
windshield, the boot or the road still smoking with tyre-
burn behind. One me gets caught by the front bumper and pulled
under the wheels. The last is dragged a good few yards before the
car finally comes to a stop, leaving a pink pencil eraser mark along
the tarmac. I witness every terrifying sensation first-hand, from
the smell of burnt rubber to the toe-squelch of blood pooling in
my boots.

But I'm fine. The me that's here, standing on the pavement, is
fine. At least that's what the driver in my reality sees. He flips me
off and keeps on driving, completely oblivious to the five other
him's and the five other me's he – they – just mowed down. It's
hard to keep track of what belongs to my reality and what belongs
to another, like getting mad at someone for something they did
in a dream. But you figure it out. And what you can't figure out
you medicate.

My hands are shaking so hard I barely manage to fish the
blockers out of my bag. Dying five times over will do that to you.
I unscrew the cap on the third try only to spill thick yellow liquid

Art: Jackie Duckworth Art

all over my jumper. Shit. No time to worry about that. I take a gulp. I hated the banana flavour at first, but now I love it. As the first mouthful slips down my gullet my heart rate slows and the fear sinks under a wave of medicated calm. I'll feel sick later but it's worth it for the relief. I shake the bottle and the last drop rolls about on the bottom. It was supposed to last me until the end of the week. Now it's decorating my sweater. I'll pick up some more tomorrow, but for now I'll have to make do.

Today's going to be shit.

"Congratulations!" The doctor said, "You have the Anxiety Gene!"

It was five days after my twenty-sixth birthday. I'd been dragged to my GP after my flatmate found me barricaded in my bedroom, a fortnight's worth of piss stored haphazardly in plastic take-away boxes under my bed. I'd been haunted by glimpses of death every day of my adult life. As I got older, they got worse. By the time my flatmate intervened I was unable to leave my bed for fear of some horrifying calamity and I'd eroded my ability to feel enthusiastic about anything, even a diagnosis.

"Count yourself lucky," he said, "We used to think it was all in your head. Now we know it's real. There's a testing window two weeks from now. Do you think you'll be free?"

I hadn't been able to hold down a job in years. Of course I was free.

I die once more on my way to work – ice on the roads – but my last gulp of blockers keeps the sensation dull and far away, like it's happening to someone else. My therapist taught me to see these alternate deaths like toy cars rushing through my mind. I'm to visualise picking them up, putting them back down, and then letting them drive away. I pick up the toy car girl on the slippery road and look at the world through her broken face. She still has a Wimpy's in her universe. Weird. Then I put her back down and she races away from me and I believe for a moment I can do this. I take a deep cold breath. I can survive a day.

I work on the first floor of a typical office building – all glass, stone and steel. Sharp, hard substances that could crack or bludgeon or cut. I avoid the wide glass staircase and head straight for the lift. I've had plenty of deaths in lifts – frayed wires, eager doors – but none on the glass stairs. Despite this, I avoid them like the plague. But today is obviously cursed, so the lifts are out. I sigh and head back to the stairs.

I hold onto the railing and take each step at a time, a nervous sweat beading the valley of my back. I can see our teenage receptionist looking at me quizzically through the glass walls of our office. I want to flash him a "fuck off" look, but I'm pretty sure the moment I take my eyes off the stairs something awful will happen. The glass will break and I'll fall to my death, or a splinter will fly up through my neck, or – and this one's the worst – I'll lose my footing, fall backwards and crack my head open on the cold glass edge of a stair below. But that'll only happen if I stop looking. As long as I'm looking at the stairs, they'll behave—

An arm hooks round my elbow.

"What have you done to yourself?"

Oh god. It's Fucking Linda.

Fucking Linda would be alright if she didn't feel the need to put herself at the centre of every story. If we're heading to the pub after work, Fucking Linda's got to turn it into an organised office outing. If our company wins an award, it has to be down to Fucking Linda's project management. And, if someone's trying to climb the stairs at their own pace, Fucking Linda's got to swoop in and save the day.

"What did you do?" She asks, "Go too hard at the gym?"

I haven't gone to a gym in years. Have you seen those running machines? Talk about a death trap.

"Thanks for the assist Linds," I grit my teeth, "But I think I've got this."

"It's ok," she says, "I don't mind."

She pulls me off balance and I trip up a stair. Not far, but enough to make me jump out of my skin. I push her off me and she knocks into one of the Support guys coming up behind us. He stumbles back, slamming his heavy backpack into the railing and spilling coffee all over his new-looking trainers.

"Christ, sorry…" Fuck. What's his name? I see him all the time but I can never remember his name. "… mate?"

He gives me this weird, hollow-eyed look, sighs and starts taking off his sodden shoes. Poor Support. They spend their days explaining basic computer functions to people who've probably never held a mouse before. Now this happens. There's only so much a person can take before they crack.

I don't know what to say so I scurry up the stairs instead, avoiding the kicked-dog look on Linda's face. She only wanted to help. It's not her fault I'm like this. But then again, it's not mine either.

The test facility was in an industrial estate just outside town. Big white building, still had that new sheen to it. I got dressed into a gown, wore bobbly wired hats and lay on whirring tables surrounded by an audience of excited doctors. Through some weird fluke of quantum-whatevers, the particles in the Anxiety Gene were entangled with particles from across the multiverse, forging brief connections between people and their alternate selves. The doctors explained that they'd seen this manifest as intrusive thoughts, visions, unshakeable feelings of dread or even elation, experiences they'd previously shrugged off as symptoms of psychosis, mania or – clue's in the name – anxiety disorders. However, in those flashes of connection, some people got glimpses of exciting worlds rich with possibility. I heard some could even have conversations with their other selves. A bloke I went to school with claimed he had this manifestation of the gene. Turned out to be bog-standard schizophrenia. Hard to tell these days.

I sat in the specialist's office hoping that the years of panic and fear would finally count for something. That I wasn't sick,

I was special. The doctor pursed her lips and asked again what I experienced. Were there any other details? A glimpse here and there but mostly just the deaths, I replied. And that was that. Other people got the special kind of the gene. The kind triggered whenever they felt a surge of excitement – of discovery, of fear, of arousal. Mine was only triggered by the flood of adrenaline experienced at the point of death. When I'm eating a sandwich and some other me in another reality chokes, when I'm crossing the road and another me gets hit by a truck, when I'm taking a shower and some other me slips and cracks her skull, that's when my gene kicks in. I got the type where I die over and over. Just my bloody luck. I was given a prescription for blockers and sent on my merry way. I'm not sure who was more disappointed, me or the doctors.

By the time I'm ready for my mid-morning coffee the blockers are wearing off. An alternate me trips on a printer cable and breaks her neck on the edge of a desk. I catch myself from the extra-dimensional fall and scream. People around me stare.

*Shit. Breathe in. Breathe out. Pick up your toy car death, look at it, put it back down, move on.*

"Sorry folks," I say, cheerfully as possible, "Stray bullet." Caitlin in Web Dev gives me a polite chuckle. I wish people would laugh about it more. Ok, it's not very funny dying over and over, but it is pretty ridiculous and that's worth a laugh at least.

My Line Manager, Mac, stops me on my way to the kitchen, "Do you have a second?" Mac's chewing on a toothpick. Does he know what havoc a swallowed toothpick can ravage on the human body? Then again, he's the type to run down stairs two steps at a time with his shoe laces untied. I once caught him digging a bagel out of the toaster with a fork.

"Well?" he asks again.

I say yes before I've had time to think and we're on our way to a meeting room before I figure out what he wants to talk about. Shit. Of course it had to be today. I'm suddenly very aware of the uneasy feeling in my stomach and the bright yellow stain down my sweater.

It shouldn't come as much surprise to hear I work as a Quality Assurance Analyst. Turns out, experiencing your death in a variety of colourful ways gives one a prodigious eye for spotting things that could go wrong. You wouldn't think you could die from laughing. You also wouldn't think you could break a website by pressing the menu button sixteen times. Well, now you know better.

However, there is such a thing as too much care.

"I'm sorry," says Mac, flicking the toothpick from one corner of his mouth to the other. I smile and assure him I understand, but in my mind all I can hear is *I didn't get it I didn't get it I didn't get it*. I'm one of the oldest members of the QA team, and the only one who's still a Junior Analyst. I knew what had done me in. I'd been testing a new banking portal. After two expensive weeks of QA, I reported back that clicking the terms and conditions page ninety-four times made the font change colour. The dev team were fascinated. The client, not so much.

Mac follows me back to the kitchen. "Are you going to be alright?" he asks, "Just I know you can get a bit –" He holds his hands out and shakes them. My gut twists in on itself.

"There was an accident this morning," I fumble with the coffee pot to give me somewhere else to look. "I ran out of meds, but I should have more tomorrow."

Mac eyes my mug and frowns. "You know…" he says.

*Oh god, not this again.*

"… I read that cutting out caffeine might help. Less stimulants, better brain chemistry."

I try to mask the frustration curdling my face. "It's not really a chemical imbalance. It's genetic. The Anxiety Gene—"

He cuts me off with a wave of his hand. "Sure, however you want to think about it."

Of course he doesn't believe me. There are a fair few who don't. It's been just long enough since the discovery for the excitement to die down, but too early for it to really affect how the everyday world works. Unless you're a quantum physicist or a neural biologist, or me for that matter, the multiverse is just another unseeable untouchable thing, like Jupiter or the Higgs Boson. I'm not surprised people question its existence, but it's mind-boggling how many claim to understand my experiences better than I do. I silently place bets on which magical lifestyle cure Mac will suggest next. Vegetables? Or exercise? He looks like an exercise guy. He wears a leather bracelet though, so maybe mindfulness.

He tilts his head thoughtfully. "I know a guy who runs courses at the Community Centre, nothing too *wooky*. Just breathing, posture, help you become more aware of your own mind."

Before I can think *Bingo*, there's a bang.

Mac's mouth hangs open and a circle of red blooms on his t-shirt.

*He's swallowed his toothpick*, I think.

Another bang and the coffee pot explodes in my hand and Mac slumps to the ground. Somewhere in another probable now, two other me's fall with him. Now the screaming starts. There are more bangs and three other me's drop to the floor. I feel every shot like a punch to the gut. I can smell blood. Both here and elsewhere. I drop behind the counter and throw my arms over my head.

*Oh shit. Oh shit.*

Gunfire rings out across desks, shattering computer screens and light fixtures, sending sparks flying. Realities fracture in my mind.

*Are we under attack? Is it terrorists?*

I look up at the dangling remains of a strip light. It strikes me as a decidedly haphazard shot.

*No. People don't shoot up offices here.*

I remember the Support guy on the stairs. The look in his eyes. The heft of his backpack. Linda's coffee on his shoes.

*Ok, maybe it could happen here.*

While my mind races, twelve alternate me's give in to temptation and peek above the counter. All twelve immediately take a bullet to the eye, the forehead, the nose. Twelve! I've never had so many before. The multitude of deaths ricochet through my brain and my thoughts scatter like marbles until I no longer know what's in my reality and what's in another. The holiday postcard on the fridge flashes five different destinations. I clutch my ears and close my eyes.

*They're just toy cars. They're just toy cars.*

I pick up each death in my mind, look it over and consider a new thought. Despite experiencing them the way I do, I'm no expert in alternate realities. I'm not sure how they come about, how they split. Is it our decisions? Or probability? Or a mix of both? In this reality the coin comes down heads, you bring a gun to work; in another reality the coin comes down tails, you leave the gun at home. It's messier than that of course. If something happens in one reality, I don't know if it means it'll turn out exactly the same in this one. But what I do know is that in twelve other realities, I looked over the counter and copped it. And in this reality, I stayed hidden and got to live.

Another me gets a bullet through the counter. I dive round the fridge just as a bullet in this reality traces the same path.

*Time to move.*

The screaming subsides. Everyone's staying quiet – either hiding or dead. Footsteps are coming this way. Time to test my theory. I slip behind the next bank of desks just as another me, one who tarried, takes a shot in the leg then five in the chest. I rarely experience deaths outside of my personal space. It's always a near-miss – getting clipped by a train, hit by a falling brick, tripping on a loose paving stone – so I know that death was a close one. Sure, I have a front-row seat for 'what *not* to do' thanks to my less fortunate alternate selves, but how many near-misses can I afford?

The footsteps prowl closer. I hold my hand over my heart, as if I'm trying to keep it quiet and stop it bursting from my chest at the same time. I edge back and my ankle bumps into something wet and heavy. I make the mistake of looking. It's Caitlin, only there's deep red hole in the back of her head. I fall back and clap my hands over my mouth. Caitlin always makes the effort to talk to me at Friday night drinks. She breeds gerbils outside of work and listens to EDM while she codes. Who'll look after her gerbils now? The horror of her death is a black hole threatening to swallow me up. But I can't fall apart, not with the shooter so close.

*It's just another death that doesn't belong to you.*

I apologise to Caitlin and put her death into a toy car in my mind. I pick her up. Look at her. Then I put her back down and let her drive away.

The footsteps leave the room and I unclasp my hands from my mouth. I need a plan, a better one than waiting for my alternate selves to cop it like Schrödinger's canaries. Do I run? Do I hide? How long will it take for the police to get here? Five, ten minutes? Let's say it's going to take fifteen minutes before some sort of official task force arrives to deal with the situation. The gunman's skulking about, like he's looking for people. I picture him hunting for me among the desks. I wonder who it could be. Angus from Finance is always the brunt of jokes at staff parties. Or then there's Dafydd in Design with his hair-trigger temper. For some reason, I keep thinking of that guy from Support on the stairs this morning. What *is* his name? I briefly wonder if there's a reality where I remember his name and he doesn't shoot up our workplace. Probably not. Point is, it's only a matter of time until I'm found.

My best chance is to get out.

The next few minutes the office is a chess board with one terrifying queen and an infinite row of pawns that look just like me. The blockers have well and truly worn off and my senses are finely tuned. I've not felt this way in years. It's like I'm a military radar for my own demise and I'm picking up all of them in state-of-the-art HD. To keep my head straight I make a check list, as if I'm QA testing a website. Move too quickly. Bang. That's a bug. So, I take my time and think. Move too slowly. Bang. Another bug. So, I make sure I don't hesitate. Stop to help someone. They cry. Loudly. Bang. Bug again. I focus on saving myself. The self in this reality. All other deaths – both my alternate selves and the bodies on the floor – are just little toy cars whizzing through my head. I pick them up, then I put them down and let them run from me, until only I remain.

I die less. I get braver. That horrible staircase comes into view through the glass boardroom and I'm so close to this being over. After a shortcut through the cloakroom I scurry under the reception desk next to the large floor to ceiling windows emblazoned with our company logo. I can see the front door downstairs through the glass, but there are no blue lights out on the street. My heart sinks. The police should be here by now. It's been at least an hour, hasn't it? I check the clock opposite the desk. It's only been ten minutes. Ten minutes and I've died fifty times at least. That's a record I'm in no hurry to break.

I'm about to make my move, when footsteps round the corner. I duck down, hoping they don't see my reflection in the glass.

But it's not the gunman.

It's Fucking Linda.

Fucking Linda stands looking at the top of the stairs, a weird faraway look in her eyes. She doesn't look hurt, but she's standing out like a sore bloody thumb. Fucking Linda's going to get herself fucking killed. I think about this morning on the stairs, the kicked-dog look on her face, and guilt twists like a key in my gut. Maybe if I'm careful, we can both get out to safety. I quickly look about, then rise out of my hiding spot.

"Hey. Linds," I whisper as loud as I can.

She looks at me, surprised. God, she must be proper out of it.

"It's ok. I think he's still inside." I step toward her, offering my hand, "Let's get out of—"

Then I see the hunting rifle tucked under her arm.

Oh. Shit. *Fucking* Linda.

Three me's run. Bang. Two me's beg. Bang. Six me's throw something at her, a chair, a book, a bag. It doesn't matter. Bang. One me defiantly flips her the bird.

Bang bang bang.

Fucking Linda watches all of this flash across my face. She lowers her rifle. "Oh," she says, "Of course. You must be having a really bad day. How many times have you died so far?"

"Honestly, I lost count on the way to work," I say.

Fucking Linda fucking chuckles.

"I didn't really figure you into the plan." She braces the rifle back into her shoulder, "To be honest, I didn't know you had it so bad. You always seem so together."

I'm trying to come up with a game plan, but I've got nothing.

"I've got very good at pretending to be fine," I say.

Fucking Linda's face darkens. "I know what you mean."

I can see the clock on the wall above her head. Eleven minutes have passed. No other me's have died in a while. I just need to play for time.

"So, what's all this…" I gesture vaguely, "… about?"

The shooty end of the rifle is pointing straight at my gut.

"You know," she says, "Out of everyone here, I think you're the only one who truly understands what it's like."

She relaxes and the rifle's aim lowers to my thigh. If she misses the artery I could survive.

"What's what like, Linds?"

"Seeing the other you's." She leans forward, like we're just sharing office gossip. "Can yours see you back? I don't think mine can. I've only got the one, thank god. I tried talking to her when I was little, but she'd never say anything back. My parents thought I had an invisible friend."

79

Fucking Linda has the fucking Anxiety Gene.

"It was fine for a while. Just me and this other Linda living our lives in tandem. Brushing our teeth, playing with our toys. Then one day, we were studying for a test in school and I stopped and watched her. I think I just wanted to see what I looked like, so I watched while she studied. Of course, the next day I failed the test and she passed. That was the first time we'd ever differed."

I lean my head to one side like I'm listening and totally not counting down the seconds before the fuzz arrive.

"No need to panic, I thought. Just got to work a little harder and then I'll be right back on track. So, when the next test came I shut myself up in my room and studied all night long. And then I slept through the exam. I'd failed. Again. Meanwhile the other Linda, my potential, was racing away from me." For a moment her gaze traces some unseen horizon, before snapping back to me. "Can you follow yours? You know, if they go some place you're not. Can you see through their eyes?"

I shake my head. I'm too scared to speak.

"I can. It's a fucking curse. I'd watch her go on day trips with my parents and hang out with my friends, while I stayed in my bedroom struggling to catch up. But it was never enough. When I got an A on an essay, I could always see the A+ on hers."

Linda puts the rifle back under her arm.

"She's this celebrity thinker type person now. Married to a paediatrician. With a beautiful house and charming friends and her first child on the way. Do you know what torture that is? To have your perfect double showing you what your life could have been, while you're stuck living the consolation prize?"

Two minutes have passed. I nod sympathetically. Come on Linda, tell me more about your fucking awful life.

"She started maternity leave this week. She was lying in bed, looking through the cards from her colleagues, making plans for the future, and she was so..." Linda takes a big shuddering breath, "... happy. That's when I understood why there's only the two of us. I'm not supposed to compete with her." She pauses.

"I'm supposed to balance her out. She's the charmed one and I'm-" she gestures at her rifle, "Well. I'm Fucking Linda. Aren't I?"

A cold feeling rises through my limbs. Fucking Linda is fucking insane.

"How does yours work again?" she asks, "Any time you die in an alternate reality you experience it here too? Is it like the uncertainty thing? Like, if I thought very seriously about shooting you in the stomach—"

Right on cue, an alternate me goes flying and I curl round my abdomen. Fucking Linda raises her eyebrows.

"Oh. Maybe you do have it worse."

I can't help myself. "You think?!"

Zero minutes. Fucking Linda's tired of fucking talking. She brings the gun back into her shoulder and aims straight at me. A shadow flits across the blinds behind her.

"On the stairs this morning, you looked so helpless. A little like you do now. Only I don't feel like helping this time." She shrugs. "Or maybe I do. Who knows? I'm feeling really indecisive lately."

The first wave of alternate bullets hit as Linda debates with herself whether or not she should shoot me. All the while, my alternate selves crumple to the floor over and over and over. I try to keep track of them all. I look them over and put them down, but they keep racing back to me, adding more each time until there are uncountable deaths around me, swirling like leaves in a hurricane. There are too many to pick up. Too many to feel separately. It's just a blur of pain and panic and terror.

So, I do the only thing I can think of.

I take all these deaths and I reduce them to one single idea. Death. My death, the one in my reality, the one that belongs to me, the one that *will* happen someday. I put death into a toy car and I look at it, without the comfort of a multiverse keeping it a whole other reality away. Then I set it down and I let it go.

And then, in that maelstrom of dying, like a word said over and over, death lost its meaning. And for the first time in years, I feel completely calm.

"Oh, so fucking what," I say. "You want to be remembered as this big scary monster? Fine. But did you have to be such a cliché? A shooting spree. Really? That's pretty basic, even for you."

Fucking Linda lets the barrel drop. She opens her mouth to say something, but I don't let her. It's my turn.

"Y'know, I've had nearly every flavour of death there is. Plane crash. Done it. Electrocution. Done it. Accidental beheading. Done it. Twice. This ride you've got me on, I've ridden it so many times I don't even bother picking up the souvenir photo anymore. I'm kind of a death connoisseur. And dying because my co-worker was too busy competing with her alternate self to succeed at her own goddamn life has got to be the dumbest one yet. Fine, shoot me. In a million other realities, a million other me's will have shaken it off by lunch time anyway."

Fucking Linda fucking falters. Not for long, but long enough.

"Oh fuck you—"

The sniper's bullet rips through her skull, spraying my face with her still-warm blood. Adrenaline courses through my veins as I watch Fucking Linda's headless corpse flop to the ground.

Black uniforms come piling into the building. I spread out my fingers. I can almost feel the pile of dead me's in a mound around my feet while I stand alone. The one who lives. I wipe the blood off my face and step away from the carnage, forgetting the glass stairs behind me.

My foot slips. Fucking Linda's blood is all over the fucking floor and now it's slicked to the bottom of my boots. I try to find traction, but my foot slips again. Blue lights flash around me. My arms windmill.

*No. Not the stairs*, I think. *Not after all this.*

I teeter on the edge, a glass line between life and death, and a million other me's in a million other realities flinch.

---

**Rhiannon Grist** is a Welsh writer living and working in Edinburgh. Her work has featured in *Strix, Fearless Femme* and *Monstrous Regiment* and has been described as "cool-as-fuck black mirror-esque". She writes and performs as part of Writers' Bloc and lives with an anatomical skeleton called Bob.

SCOTLAND'S FESTIVAL OF SCIENCE FICTION, FANTASY & HORROR WRITING

**Come along to Cymera, Scotland's first and only book festival celebrating Science Fiction, Fantasy and Horror Writing.**

**Ben Aaronovitch, Christopher Priest, Richard K. Morgan, VE Schwab, Charles Stross, Aliette de Bodard, Samantha Shannon, Claire North, Tade Thompson, Lauren James, Gareth L Powell, Ken MacLeod, Emma Newman and many, many more**

Sharpen your pencils and your wits at the Writers' Workshops

Entertain us with your work at our open mic

Dance the night away at our ceilidh

Feast your eyes on the works and publications in our creators' hall

Relish in the thrills of a Shoreline of Infinity's Event Horizon

**Friday 7th June 2019 - Sunday 9th June**

**The Pleasance, Edinburgh**

**Full details, programme  and tickets:**

**www.cymerafestival.co.uk**

**Twitter: @CymeraF**

# Fat Man in the Bardo

## Ken MacLeod

**A** **clock ticks. Somewhere, a baby cries**. You're in an oddly abstract space, all planes and verticals. It reminds you of a library. You don't remember ever being in a library. You remember nothing but the sudden unprovoked shove in the small of your back, and the precipitate drop. A split-second glimpse of shining railway tracks, wooden sleepers, the ingenious mechanism of points.

Then oblivion.

Now this.

Even here, in this Platonic afterlife, you're fat. You always will be fat. It defines you, eternally. You're the Fat Man. It seems unfair. You don't even remember eating.

Perspiring, thighs chafing in your ill-fitting suit, you set off in search of the crying baby. Your quest takes you around a corner, and at once you *are* in a library. It's no improvement: the maze of shelving seems endless. You take down a book, and find page after page of random letters. The next you open is blank, except for one page with a single flyspeck of comma.

You put the book back in its place and plod on. The crying diminishes. You cock your head, turn, walk to another corner and triangulate. Off you go again, with more confidence.

Around the next corner, at eye level, you meet pair of eyes.

The eyes are connected to a brain, which hangs unsupported in mid-air. The brain is connected to a tiny, tinny-looking audio device where its chin would be if it had a skull.

"Hello," says the brain.

"Hello," you say. You stick out your hand, then withdraw it and wipe your palm on your thigh. Hurriedly, you introduce yourself.

"I'm the Fat Man, from" – it dawns on you – "the Trolley Problem."

"Pleased to meet you," the speaker crackles. "I'm the Brain."

"Yes?"

"A Boltzmann brain," it elaborates. "A conscious human brain formed by random molecular motion in the depths of space."

"That seems improbable."

"*Highly* improbable!" the Brain agrees. "But given enough space, matter and time, inevitable – unfortunately for me." It rotates, looking around. "We seem to be in the Library of Babel, the useless library of all possible books." Its rotation brings its eyes back around to you, and stops. "I keep wishing I could *blink*."

You shrug. "Sorry, I can't help."

The Brain laughs. "Count yourself lucky you're not from the thought experiment about organ donation."

You shudder.

"Well," says the Brain, briskly, "let's see if we can find baby Hitler and calm him down. All this crying is getting on my nerves."

The Brain zooms away, and you hurry after it, your thoughts catching up at the same time. Information comes to you when you need it, yet you have no memory of any life before this. It's like you're...

But you've caught up.

"That baby is *Hitler*?"

"Yes," says the Brain, as if over its shoulder. "Time travellers keep trying to kill him. They always fail, of course, but it's most unsettling for the child. Frankly, I fear for his future mental stability."

From the next aisle comes the sound of footsteps, and a woman's voice:

"Loud and clear, Bob. Loud and clear."

You sidestep between bookcases to intercept the clicking footsteps. The woman halts. She is wearing a dark blue shift-dress and black high-heeled shoes. Over her neat hairdo sits a set of headphones with a mike in front of her mouth. She looks at you with disdain and at the Brain with distaste.

You introduce yourselves. She's Alice. She keeps talking quietly to Bob, warning him against some third-party eavesdropper, Charlie. Otherwise, she's not very communicative.

Soon the three of you find the baby crying in a carved wooden cradle in a canyon of books. You look at it helplessly, then at Alice. She shoots you a baleful glare, picks up the child, and strokes and coos and pats his back. Hitler pukes on her shoulder. Then he stops bawling, but keeps looking around. His crumpled little face glowers with wary suspicion.

Once the baby's hushed, the sound that predominates is the ticking. You listen intently, trying to detect its source. Suddenly the ticking is interrupted by a scream, followed by sobs.

"Jeez!" says Alice. "What now?"

"It's the Ticking Bomb Scenario," says the Brain. "Some poor devil is being tortured to reveal its location."

"We have to stop that!" you cry.

"Why?" asks Alice, coldly. "Do you value some terrorist's comfort over the lives of innocents?"

"*I* was innocent," you point out. "Nobody asked *my* opinion before shoving me to certain death."

You and Alice glare at each other.

"Sounds like you're a Kantian and Alice is a utilitarian," muses the Brain. "The dignity of the individual versus the greatest good of the greatest number."

Stand-off.

"I know!" says the Brain, brightly. "Let's find the Ticking Bomb and turn it off ourselves!"

"Sounds like a plan," says Alice.

The Brain rises high above the shelves, almost out of sight. It roams, rotating, then swoops back.

"Found it!" it says. "Thirty-two minutes to go before it explodes."

"Will we have time?" you ask.

"If we hurry."

Hurry, you do. Alice's heels go click-click-click. Baby Hitler bounces up and down in her reluctant embrace. You're almost out of breath. The Brain darts ahead, a gruesome will-o'-the-wisp guiding you onwards.

You arrive at a wider space amid the shelving, with a table in the middle. In the middle of the table is a box, on which is mounted some kind of apparatus. A man in a white coat is observing the box. Behind the man is another man, observing the man and the box. Behind that man stands ... well, you know how it goes.

From inside the box comes the sound of a cat mewling, a protest louder and more plaintive even than that of Baby Hitler.

"Should we— ?" you ask.

"No," says the Brain. "It would just add another layer of decoherence to the wave function."

"Damn right," says Alice. "No way am I going back for that goddamn cat."

You all hurry on, leaving Schrödinger's Cat, Schrödinger himself, Wigner, Wigner's friend and all the others to their indefinite fate. The Brain leads you around a corner and into an aisle facing a glass wall. The light is ruddy. You spare a glance outside. To the horizon stretch waste dumps, some burning. On them crawl endless human figures, salvaging junk, grubbing subsistence from garbage.

"Is that Hell?" asks Alice, sounding horrified.

"No," the Brain calls back. "It's trillions of people living lives barely worth living! But it's a better situation than mere <u>billions</u> of people living lives well worth living, wouldn't you agree?"

"No," says Alice. "I wouldn't."

"Nor I," you say.

"Too bad!" says the Brain. "The reasoning is rigorous. Your revulsion is mistaken, but understandable. It's not called the Repugnant Conclusion for nothing, you know."

You have no breath to spare for argument. Another ten minutes' jogging brings you all in front of the Ticking Bomb. The simple timer, now counting down from twelve minutes, is attached to a large cylindrical device labelled "10 kilotons".

"Oh!" says the Brain. "It's an atomic bomb! Does that change our views on the morality of torture?"

"No," say you and Alice at the same moment. Baby Hitler's eyes widen and his face brightens, but he says nothing.

Alice reaches over and turns the timer back to one hour. The ticking resumes.

"Now we have time to think," she says.

"It's interesting to reflect," says the Brain, "that somewhere in this library is a book containing a complete system of self-evident moral philosophy that answers all our questions. Formed out of random letters, just as I am formed out of random molecules."

"Along with its refutation?" says Alice.

"Point," says the Brain.

"One of us must stay here," you say, "and keep turning the clock back, while the others go and find the torture chamber before too many more fingernails are extracted. And then—"

"And then what?" asks Alice. "How does that help all the poor people outside?"

"No," you say, "but—"

"Have you noticed how our memories work? Doesn't it strike you as odd? Try drawing something at random."

You find a pen in your pocket, and a blank page in a book.

"What?" you say. "I can't think of anything I'm not thinking about."

"Tree," says Alice. You've never heard the word before. You sketch a tree.

"See?" says Alice. "That's not how human memories work. That's how *computer* memories work, as I'm sure the Brain can confirm."

"Yes," says the Brain. "And?"

"We aren't human minds," says Alice. "We're abstractions of the subjects and victims of thought experiments. This isn't a physical space, and I doubt that it's some kind of afterlife, given that none of us had *lives*. The overwhelming probability is that we're in a simulation."

"Ah," you say. "But—"

"Yes," says Alice. "What monsters the creators of such a simulation must be!"

You and Alice look out of the window at the hellish landscape, and at each other.

"We must put a stop to this," you say.

Alice nods. You reach for the timer at the same moment.

"Wait!" cries the Brain.

Too late.

Zero.

What the Brain was about to tell you is that there are worse possibilities than being in a simulation. The worst possibility is that this thought experiment *is* simply a possibility, but a logical one. From inside a logical possibility, there is no way to distinguish it from actuality. And a logical possibility can't be made or unmade by omnipotence itself, let alone by a ten-kiloton atomic bomb.

What the Brain doesn't know, and couldn't possibly tell you, is that there is a greater possibility: that somewhere, somehow, all the victims of all the logical possibilities including those that exist in what we laughingly call actuality can be saved, can be liberated, can be redeemed; that their suffering can be expunged as though it had never been; and that, however impossible that great, all-encompassing thought experiment may seem, or indeed be, it is nevertheless something for which you are doomed to strive, and to seek over and over again until you find it.

✳

A clock ticks. Somewhere, a baby cries. You're in an oddly abstract space, all planes and verticals. It reminds you of a library.

**Ken MacLeod** lives in Gourock, Inverclyde. He is the author of seventeen novels, from *The Star Fraction* (1995) to *The Corporation Wars: Emergence* (Orbit, 2017). His novels and stories have received three BSFA awards and three Prometheus Awards, and several have been short-listed for the Clarke and Hugo Awards. http://kenmacleod.blogspot.com

# And the Winner Is...

**In Shoreline of Infinity 12,** published in June 2018, we announced our second flash fiction competition, on the theme of the Moon – chosen to mark the 50th anniversary of the first landing of humankind on our Moon.

We were in awe at the variety of ways to approach this topic, and delighted that not everyone chose the Apollo route for inspiration.

Head judge Pippa Goldschmidt and the team whittled the list down to these four tales. As you have already seen Emma Levin's story *Winners* does begin with the Apollo missions, but takes us on a mischievous journey in just a few hundred words. *Superfine* by Eris Young adapts language to add to the tension and *Rabbit* by Alyssa Eckles has a good old tug at the heart strings. In the end the judging team chose Vicki Jarrett's vivid story, *La Loba*.

On you go, what are you waiting for?

*—Noel Chidwick*

# La Loba

## Vicki Jarrett

WINNER
Shoreline of Infinity Flash Fiction
Competition 2018

**We thought we'd be safer away from the city.** And, for the most part, we were right. Staying there would've been madness, but survival out here does involve sacrifice.

High up in one of the taller trees at the edge of a clearing, we get as comfortable as we can in its wide, spreading branches. The moon is rising round and full into the night sky, claiming its place among the stars. It'll be a long night. Hank stretches out with exaggerated weariness, his back the same width as the branch he's lying on. One false move is all it'd take. When I suggest he move to a safer position he sighs, shifts his shoulders a fraction and closes his eyes. Shadows gather in the lines and hollows of his face while moonlight silvers the surface, giving him the look of a tarnished icon.

It's been four weeks since Nina's last episode. We had hoped, once we were free of the hysteria gripping the city, that maybe she'd somehow be cured. Naive perhaps, but it was better than letting them take her and put her in one of those treatment facilities along with all the other girls. The ones they could catch. They say they're working on a cure. But how can that be, when they don't even know what caused the disease in the first place, or why it spread exclusively among the adolescent female population?

We never thought it would happen to our Nina. She was such a sweet child. At first it was the moods, the slammed doors, the way she'd snarl at us if we asked a simple question about schoolwork or friends. We learned to recognise the signs and back off. Well, I did. Hank never did know when to leave well alone. It was a language he couldn't, or wouldn't, begin to understand.

She started staying out late. We'd wait up, worried sick. When she came back she refused to explain herself, would fly into a rage and shut herself in her room, leaving a trail of muddy footprints through the house. The next day she'd be pale and withdrawn. She never made any effort to hide her torn and bloody clothes, simply cramming them into the laundry basket for me to wash. Hank thought this was just typical selfish behaviour but I believed it was her way of telling me what was happening to her, of asking for my help.

I stare out across the clearing, my attention snagged by movement at the edge of the wood, where the trees thicken. It could be Nina, or it could be one of the others. A substantial number of girls must have made it out of the cities as well as us. In the weeks we've been surviving out here, we've seen the signs. The blackened smudges of camp fires, shelters made from fallen branches, scattered bones.

It took me months to convince Hank we needed to leave or risk losing her altogether. He talked about his job at the council, about the mortgage on the house. Since we left, his grumbling about the day to day hardships we face has made me wonder whether he wouldn't rather have handed Nina over to the authorities and carried on with his life as though she'd never happened. I don't want to believe that, but his recent speculation that they might have cracked the science and developed a safe, viable cure by now, that it could be safe to go back, has done nothing to quieten my doubts about his priorities.

The movement in the trees comes again, from what seems to be several different places at once. There's definitely more than one of them in there. Sounds like a fight. My heart races and I have to push down the instinct to run to my daughter's defence. That wouldn't help anyone. And anyway, I can't really know whether those growling sounds are aggressive or friendly. Perhaps they're finding each other, all these lost girls, seeking strength in numbers.

The hours pass and I watch the moon cross the sky. In her light, the silver edges of the world are rivers that swell and contract, joining and separating again, always in motion. Hank murmurs in his sleep and goes to roll over. Before he manages to tip out of the tree, he is saved by some unconscious sense of balance and rights himself again. All without opening his eyes.

The moon is sinking now, the night nearly over. A pale shape is weaving through the trees, coming in our direction. Never before has she shown herself before dawn, when she usually reappears, in one piece if slightly dazed. But I've never seen her like this. I hold my breath, stay very still, and watch my daughter emerge from the shadows.

The powerful, fluid way she moves, the way her body seems to shine, not only with unmistakable health but with the same unflinching clarity as the moon. My breath escapes in a gasp. My god. She's magnificent.

How can this be a disease? Who gets to decide? Those sick old men in lab coats, injecting healthy girls with their so-called cure in their treatment centres?

She draws close and circles our tree, looking up through the branches with gleaming eyes. Even without Hank's snoring and twitching, she'd have found us. We're connected. She makes a low anxious whining noise from the back of her throat and somehow I know she hasn't fed tonight. And she must. Evolution is hungry work.

Perhaps it was always going to come to this. For every step forward there must be a shedding of what came before. I flex my feet, easing the stiffness out of my ankles, stretch out my legs and press them close to Hank's, feeling his familiar warmth. One false move is all it'd take.

**Vicki Jarrett** is a novelist and short story writer living and working in her native Edinburgh. She is the author of one novel, *Nothing in Heavy*, and a short story collection, *The Way Out*. Her second novel *Always North* is due out in August 2019 with Unsung Stories. (www.vickijarrett.com)

The BEACHCOMBER presents

STORY AND ART MARK TONER
FONTS BY BLAMBOT

HMM... SOMETHING FROM *EARTH* HAS WASHED UP ON THE *SHORELINE* OF *INFINITY.*

A YELLOW FLUORESCENT *JACKET* FROM THE *GREAT DISASTER* OF THE EARLY 21ST CENTURY.

IT *HAPPENED* AROUND *2020* IN THE *COUNTRY* THAT WAS *THEN* CALLED THE *UNITED KINGDOM.*

THE WHITE VANS

I *HOPE* THAT ELECTRICIAN IS HERE *TODAY.* I *REALLY NEED* THAT NEW SERVER RUNNING BY *TOMORROW.*

THAT'S *MAYBE* HIM THERE. *HARD TO TELL* WHEN *ALL* THE TRADESMEN DRIVE *PLAIN WHITE VANS.*

HI, CHARLIE. WHEN THE **SPARKS** GETS IN, SEND HIM **STRAIGHT** TO I.T.

WILL DO, MISS MAXWELL.

YOU **MIGHT** WANT TO CHECK ON **OLD DAVE**... HE DOESN'T LOOK **WELL** THIS MORNING.

THANKS, CHARLIE, I WILL.

HI, DAVE. READY TO INSTALL **THAT SERVER**? I **THINK** THE ELECTRICIAN IS AT THE DOOR.

WE **WON'T SEE** AN ELECTRICIAN **TODAY**, JEAN. IT'S HAPPENING AGAIN.

YOU **REALLY ARE** OUT OF SORTS, DAVE... **WHAT'S** HAPPENING AGAIN?

**JUST LIKE** BACK IN '64, THEY'RE **POURING OUT** ONTO THE STREETS ... TAKING OVER ... INVADING!

WASN'T THAT AN OLD **DR WHO** EPISODE? ... DALEKS OR SOMETHING? NOT REAL.

THAT WAS THE **OFFICIAL STORY** ... FILMING A **SCIENCE FICTION SHOW**.

BUT **I** WAS THERE ... I SAW THEM.

## Lost Part 1: Further North

# Ruth EJ Booth

Just in:
We are delighted to announce that Ruth's
Noise and Sparks column for Shoreline of
Infinity has been shortlisted for the BSFA
2018 award for non-fiction.

**As the post-Christmas nomad days** drift into the New Year – and budding enthusiasm blossoms into remorse for the self-inflicted Herculean tasks now before us – Resolution Season becomes Advice Month, where we sign up for all the courses and buy all the books that might possibly help us reach our goals.

Speculative Fiction is no exception; blogs, books, and advice columns cater to every writing issue imaginable. Even thousands of miles away in arctic Svalbard, visiting Longyearbyen for a conference, I couldn't help hearing of Cat Hellisen's new free e-book on recapturing artistic passion, *The Writer's Guide to Creative Anarchy*[1], and Gareth L. Powell's upcoming book, *About Writing* (Luna Press). With this wealth of guidance from seasoned authors, it's a wonder we ever struggle with writing.

Yet this abundance is deceptive. While such resources are helpful and encouraging, rarely does advice come tailormade. Solutions of technique may take rounds of trial and error before solving your specific problem. Forcing yourself to try what doesn't suit can feel as uncomfortable as the High Street mannequin's outfit in the Boxing Day sale.

Nowhere is this more true than in deciding how to pursue your writing. Neil Gaiman's *Make Good Art* (Headline, 2013), containing his 2012 address to Philadelphia's University of the Arts, ranks amongst the most celebrated works on this matter. Gaiman's advice on creative living touches on how he made early career decisions, visualizing his goal – becoming an author – as a mountain.

"I knew that as long as I kept walking towards the mountain I would be all right. And when I truly was not sure what to do, I could stop, and think about whether it was taking me towards or away from the mountain."[2]

It's a beautifully simple metaphor. Does that promotion bring you closer to your dream role? By all means, take it. Leading you astray? No, thanks all the same. Keeping your goal in sight helps with any career decision. There's only one problem it can't solve: what do you do when you can't see your mountain – or worse, don't know which mountain to aim for?

Some authors favour a different approach, one based on direction. Rather than heading for a goal, they focus today on values they want to embody in the future – a good work ethic, for example – and use them as compass directions in decision-making. It's a flexible path, allowing for the fact a mountain could remain unreached for many reasons – simple bad luck, for one – rather than our failures as mountaineers.

However, this still assumes you can travel in your chosen direction. When we feel blocked in our writing, that's just not possible – and to keep going may risk permanent damage to our creative abilities.

Svalbard Winters are like little else on Earth. When you land, it is in darkness: no landmarks, no ground out of your plane window – just lights suspended in the black. Even on clear days, stood outside, wrapped in layers of thermals and extreme weatherproof gear, long minutes pass as you wait for your eyes to adjust, for the mountains to conjure themselves out of the growing blue.

And Svalbard is full of mountains: great walls of rock hefted into the sky by a quirk of tectonics. What makes the landscape so dramatic brings avalanches and weather that changes from valley to valley, minute to minute. With polar bears and -20°C temperatures in Winter, Svalbard is not to be travelled lightly. In the polar night, you must know not only the terrain but what to do when the worst happens.

A couple of days in, on a tour of Longyearbyen, our guide, Henrick, related the time his snowmobile motor failed just as a storm came over. With no phone signal so far from town, there was nothing to do but dig holes in the snow, where he and his friends spent the next eight hours sheltering, hoping someone would find them.

Even when you know where you're headed, sometimes it's just not wise to go on.

✦

In *Make Good Art*, Gaiman states the best advice he received he never followed: Stephen King's response to Gaiman's early success – "This is really great. You should enjoy it."[3]

It's a bitter pill for those lost in the wilderness – to enjoy being bewildered, not knowing which way to turn. What good is celebrating the spotlight then? But maybe it's just as relevant in the dark. The only book I took to Svalbard was Rebecca Solnit's *A Field Guide to Getting Lost* (Canongate, 2005), an essay collection that celebrates being lost in all its forms. Solnit suggests that, while upsetting, being stuck can be an opportunity, a chance to take stock and explore options we might not have otherwise considered.

I was in Longyearbyen for Island Dynamics: Darkness, an interdisciplinary conference spanning subjects from architecture to zoology. I can't deny it was a jolly: I presented a paper tangentially related to my doctorate when I really should have been focussed on my upcoming progress review, a deadline I've been ignoring in favour of just trying to write again. Health problems this summer meant my Masters dissertation was a hell of last minute cramming – a road to burnout, if ever there was one.

Svalbard's darkness had a subtle character. Once a day, between 11am and 1pm, the sky at the head of the Advent valley glowed a ghost of blue, the mountains stark against it: the landscape opened up, enough for us (and our phone cameras) to appreciate its full magnificence before the sky dimmed into true night once more.

I looked forward to that time, made a point of pausing in whatever I was doing. Not because I dislike darkness, far from it: experiencing polar night, along with the aurora borealis, was my main reason for going. Yet, every day, the light brought the promise of something just beyond the mountains, the unexplored landscape. That glow fascinated me. I'd wanted to visit Svalbard for decades. I never imagined that, once I was there, I'd long for what lay beyond that horizon.

Intellectually, I knew this gloaming was no different to what I saw at home, but polar night provided just the right magical context. If I hadn't lost myself in darkness, I never would have seen the light.

Likewise, if I'd never gone to the conference, I wouldn't have had a 30-minute discussion on the Force with one scholar. I'd never have spoken with a games designer who helped me reframe a tricky aspect of my project. I'm still trying to find my way, but exploring this stuck space, I'm starting to get a sense of the blue, just over the horizon. The place where I want to be.

It's hard not to be so focussed on destinations that you fail appreciate the land you're crossing. Directions change, even mountains move. While it's frustrating being uncertain of your path, sometimes it's just a case of waiting in the dark for a little light to show up.

### Endnotes

[1] A full range of formats are linked on Cat's Facebook page here: https://m.facebook.com/photo.php?fbid=10156602332946638&set=a.121747981637.

[2] Gaiman, Neil, 'Neil Gaiman: Keynote Address 2012', The University of the Arts, https://www.uarts.edu/neil-gaiman-keynote-address-2012, paragraphs 12-13.

[3] Ibid, paragraph 43.

Ruth EJ Booth is an award-winning writer, editor, and academic based in Glasgow, Scotland. For stories and more, see www.ruthbooth.com.

# "The Future is Already Here"

## Pippa Goldschmidt

**Last year I made a journey** through the Black Forest in southern Germany. Travelling through this large and ancient forest felt like going back in time, at least until I encountered the 'Thyssenkrupp elevator tower' just outside the medieval town of Rottweil. This tower is used to develop and test the future generations of lifts, and as I saw its science-fiction metallic form rising out of the surrounding trees I was reminded of William Gibson's saying "The future is already here – it's just not very evenly distributed".

The appearance of the tower could either be experienced as jarringly inappropriate to its surroundings, or a rather exciting juxtaposition of new and old. I mention this to illustrate that technology is in itself hardly ever either completely utopian or dystopian. It is how we view it and use it, and in turn how it impacts on our lives, that makes it appear one or the other, and that in turn depends on our own views and our position within society. Utopias and dystopias are created by the interaction of technologies and societies.

First published in 1909, E. M. Forster's novella *The Machine Stops* presents a future society in which, because of some unspecified catastrophe, people live below the surface of the Earth, existing in isolated subterranean rooms and communicating with each other solely via a technology that closely anticipates the internet. All their physical needs are met by 'the Machine' (spoiler: it stops). The novella focusses on two characters who have very different responses to their world, one initially accepting, the other rebelling. For one character, the technology provides a means to utopia, the other sees this society as relentlessly dystopian. It is the changing responses to the technology that propel the story and provide the plot.

More recently, Helen Sedgwick's second novel *The Growing Season* (published last year and reviewed in *Shoreline of Infinity 10*) investigates the pros and cons of artificial wombs and their impact upon British society. Variously presented as an ingenious way of avoiding all the hard work and dangers of pregnancy and childbirth, or as an appalling Frankensteinian approach to what should remain a natural process, this is correspondingly either a utopian dream or dystopian nightmare, depending on your point of view. The novel is destined to be a modern SF classic in its detailed siting of an as-yet speculative technology (although likely (?) to become reality in the near future) in a very real and not speculative society.

One of the most interesting aspects of the novel is its even-handed approach to the technology, refusing to come down firmly on either side of the argument, this is neither sunlit uplands or grim Satanic mills. It simply and persuasively argues that this technology can be both utopian and dystopian at the same time, depending on who uses it.

When we read fiction, the made-up worlds we explore trigger true emotions which are identical to the ones we feel in the real world. By reading novels (of any genre) we enter into the heads of the fictional characters; we understand why a bored housewife in nineteenth century rural France might take first one lover and then another, before committing suicide. Or why an under-used and under-appreciated robot might also feel suicidal. Fiction seems to have an extraordinary power to engender empathy in its readers. This empathy allows us to

**"Philip K. Dick's women characters almost invariably come across as somewhat less human than his replicants"**

understand how the characters respond to and are affected by the real or make-believe technology in their worlds. It helps build a bridge between their worlds and ours, and helps us see the many different impacts of technology. But. There is a big BUT. Too many fictional investigations of technology have been limited by the authors' unexamined prejudices. Philip K. Dick's women characters almost invariably come across as somewhat less human than his replicants. More generally, the authors who dominated SF in the 20th century could not conceive of technologies being used to answer problems that women faced, because they were on the whole blind to those problems.

The argument has been made many times but it's worth making again, if we want SF to continue to provide some insights into future societies, we must do all we can to enable SF to be written and published by as wide a cross-section of writers as possible. If only certain types of people in certain societies write SF, then that SF will only solve those people's problems.

**Pippa Goldschmidt** is the author of the novel *The Falling Sky* and the short story collection *The Need for Better Regulation of Outer Space*. She likes thinking and writing about the universe. Her work has been broadcast on Radio 4 and appeared in a variety of publications including *A Year of Scottish Poetry* and the *New York Times*.

How would you measure the height of someone half-horse, half-human?

In centaur-meters

—*Lisa Timpf*

Three chrononauts caught in a time loop walked into a bar...
...walked into a bar...
...walked into a bar...
...walked into a bar...
...
—*Ian McKinley*

# Neil Williamson

## Chris Kelso

**If you know your science fiction** (specifically your Scottish SF) you probably know the name Neil Williamson – and if you don't, you really should. Neil is the widely-regarded as the 'gentleman scholar' of the Scots SF scene. I feel confident saying that if you see him at an event, don't be afraid to approach him; he is more generous with his time than many writers who have achieved half his legacy. For one of our most highly-decorated writers – who's been nominated at various times for the British Science Fiction Association, British Fantasy Society and World Fantasy awards in his career – Neil remains disarmingly unassuming. But it's no secret that Mr. Williamson relishes a pint and chat as much as he relishes portraying the falcate monoliths of some distant Martian cityscape.

Something else that should be said before we even get to the man's fictional yield, is that he is very encouraging of young writers. A few years ago, following a reading of mine which went down like a steampunk balloon, I will always remember Neil coming up to me and offering a consolatory word:

"You had some beautiful imagery in there. The mics were pure shite, mate."

And that simple kindness helped a lot.

Geniality aside, Neil is a wicked good writer.

Neil's writing always has a fascinating musicality to it. He writes with harmony and timing in mind, but stories like *Sweeter Than* have a core interest in how music can alter consciousness. *Sweeter Than* proffers an interesting hypothesis – what if your entire life really had a soundtrack? You meet someone and joyful violins soar and swell. Melancholy instrumentals drift in to accompany a loss. Music seems important to Neil (he is, after all, a musician in his non-SF-writing spare time) and this fixation bleeds into his work. *Arrhythmia continues this theme of music, of dancing to the same beat, and how disruptive influences can disturb the rhythm and flow of conformed society.*

Shoreline's featured story, *The Death of Abigail Goudy,* is another example of Neil drawing on his musical stimulus. We think you'll really enjoy it.

His first novel of two so far, *The Moon King* is a fantastic place to start for any newbie. Set beneath a captive moon in the fictitious city of Glassholm (and mirroring the writer's own city of Glasgow), the disparate denizen become interlinked in an ingenious way. *The Moon King* is a deep cleansing-bath-of-a-novel, full of melodic prose and resonant emotional brio – and in it is all the tenderness and musicality of the man himself. Neil's second novel is *The Memoirist* (2017), an Orwellian rock memoir-cum-dystopian chef-d'oeuvre, that will win the hearts of even the stuffiest science fiction reader.

Neil has also published two collections of short stories: *The Ephemera* (2006) and *Secret Language* (2016) and co-edited the anthologies *Nova Scotia: New Scottish Speculative Fiction* (2005, with Andrew J Wilson) and *Thirty Years of Rain* (2016), with Cameron Johnston and Elaine Gallagher.

Other stories worth checking out are: *The Insider* (published in Imposter Syndrome anthology, edited by James Everington and Dan Howarth) – a chilling tale of cyber-fraud in the Black Mirror vein, and *The Euonymist* (which can be found archived in Electric Velocipede's online fiction database) – a family-drama about a planet-namer called Calum.

Tell him you like his work next time you're chatting over a pint.

# Chris Kelso talks to Neil Williamson

**CK: Tell us about your journey as a writer.**

**NW**: I've been a reader since I was young and I've always been imaginative but, aside from school exercises, it took me until adulthood to start experimenting with actually writing fiction. Inspired by discovering Interzone magazine when I lived in London, so when I returned to Scotland I enroled in Duncan Lunan's Glasgow University evening class on writing SF and Fantasy, which led in turn to my joining the Glasgow Science Fiction Writers' Circle. And that's where I wrote my first stories.

My first sale was to *Territories* magazine, edited by fellow GSFWC member, Gary Gibson, and my next was the first of several I sold to Andy Cox's *The Third Alternative* (precursor to *Black Static*). A while later, I made a start on a novel called *The Moon King* and signed with John Jarrold to be my agent. The novel didn't sell initially despite going through several revisions and, while that was happening, I went back to short fiction. In 2005 Andrew J Wilson and I edited a book called *Nova Scotia: New Scottish Speculative Fiction* to showcase Scots writers at the Glasgow Worldcon that year and we were surprised and delighted when it was shortlisted for the World Fantasy Award. The following year my first collection, *The Ephemera*, was published by Elastic Press (it was later rereleased with extra stories by Infinity Plus Books).

During that period I began to be asked by Ian Whates to contribute short stories to his NewCon Press anthologies and at one point he also enquired about a novel. After another round of editing, *The Moon King* was published in 2014. NewCon have subsequently been incredibly good to me, subsequently publishing my second collection, Secret Language in 2016, and my SF novella, *The Memoirist*, last year.

My most recent project was editing, with Cameron Johnston and Elaine Gallagher, *Thirty Years of Rain*, an anthology to celebrate the thirtieth anniversary of the Glasgow SF Writers' Circle.

**CK: Did you have another life before writing?**

**NW**: I have several other lives as well as writing! I've got a nine to five-day job and I'm a musician and cabaret performer.

**CK: How important is Scotland to you?**

**NW:** I'm not sure how to answer that. Scotland isn't a perfect country, and I'm not the type that gets misty eyed and can't see its faults, but there's lots I love about it. At the moment I especially love the small-S socialism expressed as a desire for inclusivity and fairness for all who live here – which is not to say that those qualities aren't evident elsewhere in the UK, just that they are often overwhelmed by predjudices stoked by fear. It's an unfailingly beautiful place to live too.

**CK:Do you have any plans to release a novel/short story?**

**NW:** I've sold two short stories so far this year which should appear over the coming months. Both are a bit out there (which made them fun to write). One will appear in an anthology of far future fairy tales called Once Upon A Parsec (NewCon Press) and the other is slated to appear in The Jackal Who Came In From The Cold (Fox Spirit), an anthology of spy stories featuring anthropomorphic animals and furries. On top of those, I'm finishing off a space fiction novella for Stone Owl Stories called *The Packet* and the final story for a new collection of near-future SF stories.

On the novel side of things, the sort-of prequel to *The Moon King* is currently with publishers. And the novel I'm about to start is a noirish heroic fantasy about poison, lies and enduring love.

---

**Chris Kelso** is an award-winning genre writer, illustrator, screenwriter, and anthologist. His work has been published in *Black Static, Locus, Daily Science Fiction, Antipodean-SF, SF Signal, Dark Discoveries, The Lovecraft* e-zine, *Sensitive Skin, Evergreen Review* and many others. He has been translated into French.

# The Death of Abigail Goudy (extract)

## Neil Williamson

"**Jean-Baptiste Lully died from a conducting injury**." She offered me this while clambering upon the outcrop that she'd gleefully christened the clit for the way it protruded at the base of the narrow vee-shaped pasture and overhung the gushing waterfall below.

"Really?" The rock was slick with spray but I refrained from warning her about it. I'd already made that mistake once. She said I sounded like her dad.

Abi reached down for the flags. "Lully was a court composer for the Sun King. In the days before they had conductors' batons, they used a heavy staff to keep time." She stepped onto the highest part of the rock, wobbled, and then righted herself, with the furled flags outstretched to the sides like a tightrope walker. She grinned down at me and I was momentarily dazzled by the spray and the alpine sunshine. "So there he was, beating away on his big gilded staff, and he only went and bashed his foot. The wound festered, then duly turned gangrenous. Fin de Lully." She had her poise now, like a gymnast about to perform some feat of acrobatics. "Well...?"

"What?"

She nodded towards the recording equipment waiting up the hill and I scurried off obediently. When I was in position, she raised the flags above her head. The silk fluttered like emerald sails. Then she waved them and that was the signal for me to set the recorder going, and for the tenor and the violinist a little higher up the meadow to begin their performance, and for the patient, bemused Austrian farmer way up in the high pasture to start bringing his herd down the mountainside.

Once everything was underway we lay in the grass and listened to the birdsong and the rushing water and the approaching clatter of cowbells, and to the twin melodies of Abi's music rising into the spring air, shimmering off the mountains that ringed our little valley, colouring the air with echoes.

We weren't a couple. We never were that. But lying in that field with the wildflowers and the insects and sounds of nature and music mixed together in that huge, natural echo chamber, we were happy.

Something hovered and droned near my head until Abi swatted it gently away. "Did you know Alban Berg died from a bee sting?" she whispered.

This is an extract from the short story 'The Death Of Abigail Goudy' in *Secret Language*
Published by NewCon Press
www.newconpress.co.uk

# REVIEWS

When I travel for work, the size of the bag I take with me is directly proportional to the number of books I want to take with me. Because reading time, honest to goodness, no interruption, reading time, is a rare and precious commodity. So if you are as time poor as most people are, you've got to wonder if all those Game of Thrones type tomes are worth the investment. Why start book one if book four is a turkey? Well this season, SOI readers are here to help! We've tackled entire trilogies, sagas and anthologies and selected a beautiful bushel to share with you all. Enjoy!

—*Sam Dolan, Reviews Editor.*

## Worlds and Beings
**Edited by Horia Gârbea**
**Published by Romanian Cultural Institute**
**Review by Eris Young**

*Worlds and Beings* is a large collection by any standard. Weighing in at 25 authors and even more stories, the book offers a huge range of voices, which might come as a surprise to readers who don't tend to seek out translated fiction. The anthology is mostly science-fictional, but many of the pieces push the boundaries of the genre, as if to ask why we draw those very boundaries where we do. The diversity of the collection is its greatest strength: an eclectic mix of hard and soft sci-fi, surrealism and magical realism makes *Worlds and Beings* more like a buffet than a ten-course meal, it is full of treats that can be sampled at the reader's leisure, and each piece can be appreciated separate from the others.

The range of styles, voices and themes in *Worlds and Beings* is impressive: some are short and sharp as a captain's log and others are as friendly and rambling as a yarn

WORLDS AND BEINGS
Romanian Contemporary
Science-Fiction Stories

spun over a glass of wine. Many of the stories in the collection are set in the Romania of the past, present and future but just as many look outward, towards far-flung universes and ambiguous liminal spaces. Some of the pieces are more thought experiment than story, contemplations on everything from art to technology to historical revisionism, and many have endings playfully lacking in closure, causing the reader to question their own preconceptions about form and plot structure.

There are unifying threads and parallels, of course: 'Grey-Ray. The Duty' by Michael Haulică plays with Western indie popular culture as deftly as 'Flight Over the Silent Mountain' by Dănuţ Ungureanu does with modernist art. A particular wry wit permeates many of the pieces, poking fun at everything from Soviet isolationism to serial murder.

At the same time, there is a darkness to a great many of these pieces, a bleakness of outlook that doesn't just limit itself to one theme or subject matter: A Spanish conquistador desperate for gold is bent on wiping out an indigenous civilisation. Mysterious artefacts are the only traces left of hundreds of stranded, unwilling time travellers. A mysterious compound acts as a detention centre for metahumans whose gifts make them too dangerous to live in society. Many of the protagonists in these stories meet gruesome ends and perhaps even more are faced with existential questions and dilemmas that are just as chilling. None of these stories could be mistaken for escapism.

Several of the pieces in Worlds and Beings stood out particularly to me: Rodica Bretin's 'The Bride from the Garden' surprised me with its emotional depth and the subtlety with which it draws the relationship between the protagonists and the people they have known. I found

the unflinching realism with which Liviu Radu draws his protagonist in 'El Dorado' refreshingly unapologetic. The quotidian unreality of Lucian Ionică's 'Among Other Mornings' sent a shiver down my spine, and the visceral, even gruesome imagination of 'All of the Remaining Days,' by George Lazăr, stayed with me long after I finished reading.

Worlds and Beings isn't a perfect collection: overall the book has a slightly rough-and-ready feel to it, and the cover design has a decidedly indie flavour. Both of these factors might put off readers who are used to reading slick, minimalist books with huge marketing budgets, but if I know the market, readers of old pulp sci-fi and crowdfunded or self-published anthologies may be drawn to Worlds and Beings for these very features.

And if Worlds and Beings is a little rough around the edges, this is because it is a pioneering work of art. Never before have this many Romanian science fiction stories been made available to such a wide anglophone audience; even this fact alone should make the collection worth reading. Sci-fi fans have long had their fingers on the pulse of underground publishing, and a sense for the weird-and-wonderful. Many of us have trawled garage sales for obscure eighties paperbacks, or traded longform Star Trek fanfiction scrawled margin-to-margin in school copybooks. This book is for those readers: the readers who are loyal to the genre, and not afraid to get their hands a little dusty.

Slightly more worrying, though, is the fact that of all 25 authors, only four are women and only three were born after 1970. There are a number of reasons why this might be, and I don't know enough about Romania to make an educated guess. Perhaps girls have been discouraged from writing genre fiction, or chased away (as many female readers of SFF throughout the world have been) by male gatekeepers trying to keep their genre "pure". Perhaps the author population is ageing because younger people are less likely to get published. Many of the authors are journalists or scientists: perhaps people without degrees or qualifications are less likely to be published as well.

I imagine many of the reasons for the skewed author lineup are the same that have limited the diversity of English-language sci-fi and fantasy until very recently. And in the same way that I see more diverse authors being published in English-language sci-fi in recent years, so too do I have hope that the authorship of future anthologies (and I hope there will be future anthologies) of this kind will also become more diverse as time goes by. If the range featured in just this collection is anything to go on, when that happens the English-speaking world will be taken by storm.

## How to Fracture a Fairy Tale
Jane Yolen
Tachyon Publications
298 pages
Review by Laura Gregory

Fairy tales provide a connection across generations, cultures, and mediums. From the historic, often gruesome origin, to the Disney™-fied movie versions, they become a touchstone of common narrative through childhood memories. In this collection of short stories, Jane Yolen's fairy tales have been repackaged for the modern reader, drawn together by an introduction by another modern fairy tale "fracturer", Marissa Meyer of Cinder fame. The way Yolen creates the breaks is looking at the original material through a new lens, whether that be a different character point of view, a modern setting, or the collision of two or more myths. While the source material will be familiar to most, the prolific fantasy author adds a

creative spin and original contribution to each one. With a title of How to Fracture a Fairy Tale, the reader is also provided with advice on how to take a crack at examining the old stories from new angles. Yolen fans may have read some of these short stories in other publications, however there is new content in the Notes section at the back of the book, where Yolen reflects on how she approached each short story and includes an additional poem inspired by the work.

'The Bridge's Complaint' is based on '3 Billy Goats Gruff' and shows the originality of selecting a point of view character that is an essential part of the original tale, but had no voice or agency within it. In this quirky retelling, the bridge is not only cognizant of the trolls and goats criss-crossing across its span, but actually inadvertently contributes to the troll's demise. Reading about the desires and experiences of a bridge's life creates a character out of a plot mechanism and with fairy tales littered with glass slippers and poison apples, it makes one wonder

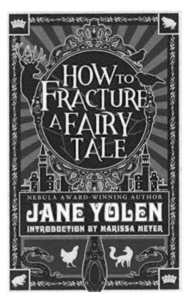

how many other tales of inanimate objects are just waiting to be told.

'Cinder Elephant' is a more contemporary twist on 'Cinderella', but the period setting is unclear, because there are still princes and royal balls, but also football, baseball and golf. It has a feisty narrative with two bratty stepsisters and, while the setting is modern-ish and the title heroine is heavyset, it feels less a reimagining of the original tale as a superficial gloss on top of the standard tropes. But then that is the nature of working within established fairy tales, they at once becomes a jumping off point as well as a constraint. Veer too far from the original tale and then one has to wonder if it is still considered "fractured" or just new work. Another Cinderella inspired story in this collection is 'The Moon Ribbon', which starts similarly with a soot-covered maiden and then breaks out into an unique story with its own intriguing magical elements and atmosphere of mystery. There is a warm bond between mother and child that helps counter the evil step-mother and step-sisters and subverts the traditional ending of her having to rely on marriage to a prince to escape her fate.

'Slipping Sideways Through Eternity' is a powerful story that comes about from a mash-up of Yolen's own novel The Devil's Arithmetic and, as Yolen explains in the Notes, "an entirely different take on the role of Elijah in the stories from Jewish tradition." Being unaware of the source material, I had no familiar reassurances of happily ever after as the story follows the protagonist as she travels back in time to a WWII era concentration camp. The details are vivid without the sheen of fantasy to soften them and while the ending is hopeful, the bittersweet story adds a resonate depth to the anthology.

How to Fracture a Fairy Tale is a catchy title but falls a little short to encapsulate the extent of folklore, myth and legend that is actually contained within its pages. When Yolen encourages the reader to imagine their own way to fracture a fairy tale, it leaves hope that there will be future stories that will cross diverse lines and cultures and perhaps break the mould of the protagonist always being a Princess and the evil parental always being the Step-Mother. Overall this collection ties in nostalgia of fairy tales of memory while invoking a desire to read the original material and track how far the tales have been twisted into the collective consciousness and hopefully will encourage the reader to make an attempt to fracture their own favourite tale.

## Watching the World Burn
**The Plague Trilogy:**
**1. A Lovely Way to Burn (2014)**
**2. Death is a Welcome Guest (2015)**
**3. No Dominion (2017)**
**by Louise Welsh**
**Published by John Murray**
**Review by Iain Maloney**

There are two kinds of SF: that which is mainly interested in ideas and that which is interested in people. Asimov's Foundation series lays the emphasis more on ideas than characters. Margaret Atwood's The Handmaid's Tale is explicit in the title: it's about Offred first and foremost. Every story is a balance of the two, but it's always an unequal balance, and each reader has their own preference. I'm more in the Atwood camp. This is why, for me, the greatest SF writer is John Wyndham.

The ideas are brilliant, but it's the people thrown into these bizarre events that are the heart of his stories. Radio script editors, suburban families, young children. They are people like us, thrust into end-of-the-world events, alien invasions, being stalked

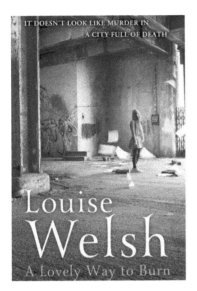

by cooperative spiders. We are forced to confront how we would respond: Would we break down? Would we have the gumption to fight back? Would we find a pub and wait for the whole thing to blow over?

All of this is a long way to explaining why Louise Welsh's *The Plague Trilogy* so neatly landed in my wheelhouse. The three novels – *A Lovely Way to Burn*, *Death is a Welcome Guest* and *No Dominion* are end-of-the-world dystopias in that everyman Wyndham tradition – the extraordinary careering into the every day.

*A Lovely Way to Burn* starts with Stevie (Stefanie) Flint being stood up. Stevie is not the kind of person who gets stood up and goes to find out what the hell her partner, Simon, thought he was up to. Turns out (no particular spoiler here) he's dead, apparently one of the first victims of "the Sweats", a plague-like epidemic with flu-like symptoms that very quickly sweeps the world bringing civilisation to its knees.

Welsh is primarily known for her crime fiction and that's how she approaches her slide into science fiction – *A Lovely Way to Burn* is a whodunit set against the backdrop of the end of the world. It's a very Asimovian splicing of genres and one that works well on a number of levels.

Firstly, it keeps things focused on Stevie. Her conviction that Simon was murdered is the spine of the novel, not the end of days. It gives her direction and drive, and keeps her moving around London when any sensible person would either hit the Winchester or get out of Dodge.

As a murder mystery it's up there with Welsh's best: well-plotted and as twisty as you could hope for. The epidemic adds a hectic dimension missing from most crime thrillers – just getting to and from the events and encounters that unravel the mystery are fraught with danger. It's a frenetic page-turner that does ample justice to both genres, and could be the perfect crossover.

*Death is a Welcome Guest* moves the cataclysm on a stage. We're still in London, this time with up-and-coming comedian Magnus McFall (Welsh does a nice turn with RL Stevenson-esque nominative determinism: Stevie is hard as flint. McFall: (n) the Scottish apocalypse). After a hard day's night Magnus intervenes to prevent a rape and is mistaken for the perpetrator, arrested, and banged up. When his cellmate develops flu-like symptoms, you know there's no way this will end well. Cue a prison break and a charge across country with Magnus's Orkney home as the ultimate destination.

This is much more in post-apocalyptic SF territory and many of the set-pieces and tropes Welsh deploys are familiar. The middle part of a trilogy is often the most difficult to balance: the world is already set up and you're only going some way towards a conclusion, a narrative *coitus interruptus*. Welsh sidesteps that by ditching Stevie entirely. We start again with Magnus, get a new perspective on a story that was the backdrop to book one and is now the foreground of book two. While Stevie stayed to solve a crime, Magnus, accused of one, flees as fast as his stolen motorcycle will carry him. It's a clever piece of storytelling, allowing the apocalypse to roll on and broaden out while keeping us firmly rooted in a single, personal story.

The frenetic pace of the first book is cranked up here, the propulsion of the murder plot replaced by a headlong charge along Britain's B roads. Welsh's writing has followed a similar trajectory. Always someone who pays close attention to the heft of a sentence, her writing has become tighter, leaner, pacier over the years. Each volume of this trilogy is pushing 400 pages but at no point does Welsh take her hand off the throttle: it's the end of the world as we know it, and no one is going to feel fine.

By *No Dominion*, there is barely an ounce of fat on the bones of either the book or the characters. I have to admit to finding this the most difficult to read. This is not a criticism of the book – it's testament to how terrifying, claustrophobic and unrelenting the story had become. Like Joey reading *The Shining* in *Friends*, I needed to put the book in the freezer and cool off.

We open on Orkney, seven years after the events of book two. Few native islanders survived but others found their way from the mainland and a peaceful community of sorts has been created. Stevie Flint is the democratically elected President of Orkney, Magnus a sullen and, when possible, drunken constituent. The focus, right from the start, is the next generation. Children who were very young when the Sweats came are now approaching adolescence. When strangers arrive on Orkney, it triggers a series of events that threatens the community and forces Stevie and Magnus to return to the mainland.

If books one and two were Britain

falling apart, book three is a survey of the pieces. As Stevie and Magnus head south they pass through pockets of fundamentalism and feudalism on their way to Glasgow, where a fascist "New Corporation" is in its early days. Wherever they go, violence meets them. The world has gone to shit, humanity reverting to base drives. It is a journey into the heart of darkness and while the climax of this trilogy is dramatic and emotionally draining, you know it's never going to be happy.

*The Plague Trilogy* is everything great SF should be: exciting stories, captivating ideas, deep new worlds and real, recognisable characters. It nestles perfectly into that John Wyndham/Margaret Atwood tradition of the real colliding with the unreal. It is also a strong addition to the growing corpus of Scottish dystopia (see *Shoreline of Infinity* 8½ for more). While I've long been a fan of Welsh's crime fiction, I sincerely hope that she isn't done with SF yet.

*An interview with Louise Welsh about The Plague Trilogy will feature in the next issue of* Shoreline of Infinity.

## Binti Trilogy
**Binti**
**Binti: Home**
**Binti: The Night Masquerade**
**By Nnedi Okorafor**
**TOR 2015/2017/2018**
**Review by Samantha Dolan**

When a series is a Hugo and Nebula award winner, expectations are set. When the blurbs are written by Neil Gaiman, Veronica Roth and juggernaut Ursula K. LeGuin, your interest is well and truly piqued. And when you quit trying to pronounce the authors name even in your own head, you're ready for the journey that is *Binti*. You'll quickly realise that there's no point in trying to impose your own understanding of any world on this one because as quickly as you make a decision, Okorafor will knock it from your grasp.

Lets deal with the obvious first. Science Fiction is not often seen as the province of BAME people. And Nnedi Okorafor hasn't attempted to hide her Nigerian heritage at all. Binti is pictured proudly with her Himba roots on display on the cover of each of these books. So what does that tell us about what we're about to read? Firstly, that you're going to get a masterclass in what it feels like to be other. For some people, it'll be your first taste of what it could mean to be third culture kid. But beyond that, the skill of people like Okorafor and N.K Jemisin is that the ethnicity of their protagonists is not the story they're trying to tell. Ethnicity is a background colour, a lens through which the reader can experience the world. For some, that lens will be sharper than a magnifying glass, for others, beer goggles. But the world, no, *universe* that Binti inhabits is so exquisitely detailed, so fantastical in its scope, that you can't help but be swept along with it.

The trilogy begins with the juxtaposition of a technological advancement and Himba tradition. Binti is a teenage girl who is going against the fundamental teachings of her people. The Himba retreat within, within their village and within themselves, but Binit has been accepted to the prestigious Oomza University. She was leaving, to find out what her potential really was, in the wee small hours of the morning, against the advice and blessing of everyone she had ever known. In those first moments, Binti is told by the equivalent of the Customs agent that she was the pride of her people. But Binti knew better.

This first instalment takes place almost entirely on a living ship called the Third Fish which is carrying a host of other students and professors to Oozma. Binti might be the only Himba on the ship but she's not rejected. She's a curiosity but she speaks the same mathematical language as the other students. What she can do, called 'treeing', with formulas induces meditative states that allow the mind to experience the freedom it needs to solve problems. Binti is also a harmoniser, like her father, and she uses her treeing ability to reconcile differences in the universe. This ability it central to Binti and the story that follows.

The other central tenant is war, an interplanetary war between the Khoush (the closest to humans we could define) and the Meduse, who in my head are giant floating jellyfish though I'm embarrassed to reduce

them to so few words. On the journey to the university, Third Fish is attacked by the Meduse and everyone is killed bar Binti, who is saved by an artefact she'd found in the desert near her home. I've barely scratched the surface of a story that lasts about 84 pages. This story is lean, tight and compelling and slides confidently into *Home*.

*Biniti* took our protagonist out into the stars and the second instalment is not subtly named. We follow Binti and her Meduse partner Okuw back to Earth. After a year at the university, making otjize (the clay that gives the Himba people their beautiful reddened skin tone) from alien clay, Binti feels the pull of the home to partake in a pilgrimage. It's fascinating to watch Binti struggle with her identity. At the university, it's so clear that's where she's supposed to be. And yet her upward blossoming is also propelling her roots to tunnel as deep into her traditions as possible. She isn't sure of the welcome she'll receive, especially with the changes that have happened to her, but she can't ignore the call. A pregnant Third Fish happens to be the ship taking her home and Binti has to struggle with the grief and trauma of what happened the first time. The strongest part here for me was watching Binti employ all the tools of her grief counselling. Sometimes it worked, sometimes she spiralled into a panic. I'm sure anyone with first hand knowledge of dealing with grief would recognise the cycle. The other part *Home* that really resonated was when Binti, who was welcomed by her family at the port, chose to wear a dress she'd found at university down into the kitchen and she's effectively heckled for looking ridiculous. It brought back memories for me of being heckled by my aunts at family parties. Or think of *My Big Fat Greek Wedding*. People with large families will know that however big or fancy you get, they'll always be there to remind you of your place. But unbeknownst

to Binti, her home is not just the Root, her ancestral family home, but amongst a people she's never seen as anything other than savages.

Through *Home* and into *The Night Masquerade*, the reader joins Binti as she assimilates all she was into who she is and who she could become. It's not an easy journey and the first 50 pages of the third instalment is quite disorientating to read, intentionally so. Our harmonizer is described as 'broken' because she's brought discord with her. The Khoush and Meduse are back to the brink of war and it's happening on her land. She's told repeatedly that it was only a matter of time but who she is, the life she's trying to craft for herself, has given an opening to free the very worst in both sides. Intentionally or not, she had brought doom with her and Binti takes it upon herself to live up to her potential and solve the issue. And for a moment, it looks like she's done it and it's a little disappointing from a reader's perspective. But then you realise that there's at least a third of the book left to go and Okorafor isn't done knocking you out.

I really enjoyed this series. There isn't an extraneous page in the lot. The entire story has been pared right down to the essentials and in doing so, the world building proved to at least double the size. The three books only just break the 400 page mark. That's not even part one for George R.R. Martin. And yet there's no doubting the development of the characters. Binti evolves again and again in a very external way but so do all young (and old) adults as we figure out who we are and who we want to be. And I enjoy an author who doesn't feel the need to boil things down the lowest common denominator. Though if there is any flabbiness in these stories, it is in the repetition of the Himba traditions, the Meduse stance on honour, how Binti 'trees'. It's more in the *Night Masquerade* because it's three years after the release of the first book but I don't think the story would have suffered for allowing the reader to just recall those details. The Night Masquerade as a story line is also a little loose. It's a 'twist' of the M. Night Shyamalan ilk and it doesn't massively add anything to the story. But those are tiny niggles in a transformative series. The Binti trilogy sings proudly across the cosmos and I for one am very keen to read anything else this author chooses to pen.

## A Practical Guide to the Resurrected
ed. Gavin Miller & Anna MacFarlane
Freight Books - distributed by The New Curiosity Shop/Shoreline of Infinity Publications
198 pages
Review Megan Turney[1]

I tend to find it a struggle to write about a book that I've really enjoyed; this usually happens with those texts that have been so absorbing that it becomes a bit overwhelming trying to gather my thoughts and write anything even remotely eloquent enough to do the book justice. It is indeed for this reason that I've been unsuccessfully attempting to write about the short story collection *A Practical Guide to the Resurrected*. I flew through all 21 stories, with each as thrilling and alarming as the last. The idea for the collection began as a competition funded by The Wellcome Trust and held by the University of Glasgow. With over 600 entries, and only 20 winning places (as well as a bonus story by award-winning author Adam Roberts) it's no surprise

that this book is as outstanding as it is. The submissions have been inspired by an academic project that sought to highlight the connection between 'science fiction and the medical humanities.' The stories generally explore society's tumultuous relationship with our health, the complex notion of humanity, and the increasingly complicated desire to improve our bodies; all of which are uncomfortably identifiable characteristics in a society that feels as if we're progressively more dependent on the technology we create.

In their introduction, the editors Gavin Miller and Anna McFarlane outline how they've been motivated by their desire to increase the recognition of 'the medical humanities in shaping the future of medicine, and as complementary to biomedical research'. However, an interesting undercurrent to the collection is the shared tendency to focus less on the specific biomedical developments involved. Instead, the authors collectively stress the often-harrowing emotional effects and the fundamentally human reactions that come as a result of that new technology, much of which is worryingly conceivable. With this core feature being so innately relatable, and as something that could arguably become ever more realistic as our medical research advances, the stories have the potential to appeal to such a varied readership. In addition, the winning authors come from an array of diverse backgrounds, spanning the globe from Nigeria to New Zealand, from doctors and professors to creative writers and journalists, providing further proof that they can be accessed and enjoyed by more than just those involved within the medical profession.

The broad range of writing styles are also evocative of several popular science fiction authors too; comparable to the skill of Margaret

1    Disclaimer: the reviewer did not know that this collection would be distributed by Shoreline of Infinity - honest!- *Ed.*

Atwood, Ursula K. Le Guin, Greg Egan, Ted Chiang and Philip K. Dick, to name just a few. But that is not to say that these stories weren't original. I've read a fair amount of science fiction that considers the same kind of themes covered in this collection - some successful, and some not. Yet, I can easily say that all the winning authors have managed to approach their topics in such a provoking, creative way, and in so few pages, that I find myself still thinking about them days after putting the book down.

So, I can certainly empathise with competition judge, Adam Roberts, in the difficulty he found having to re-read and re-rank his favourites; it was a very 'close-run thing' for me too. For Roberts, his final decision ranked Seth Marlin's 'A Practical Guide to the Resurrected' in first place, Marija Smit's 'His Birth' as second, and Peter McCune's 'Blisstec Ltd.' as third. Although I do agree that these three were deserving winners, there were a few other stories that were just so ingenious and haunting that they became prominent favourites of mine. Included in this list, I'd like to mention:

Hazel Compton's 'System Stable'
Maija Haavisto's 'The House She Grew'
Okaimame Oyakhirome's 'Doctor 213'
EA Fow's 'The Anthalopus Cure'
Alyson Hilbourne's 'Frozen to the Core'.

Finally, A Practical Guide to the Resurrected delves into a such multitude of significant issues that I've not even managed to touch upon in this review. And, although I'd love to probe and discuss every aspect of every short story, as there really is so much to consider, it's for the best that I refrain from revealing too much and allow other readers to discover this dynamic collection for themselves. Therefore, as must be abundantly clear by now, I would recommend this book to any science fiction reader, or any reader looking for a disturbingly relevant, thought-provoking text. With such diversity and talent, there is bound to be at least one story in this collection that has the captivating effect they've all had on me.

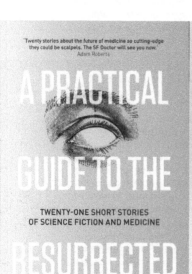

Twenty stories about the future of medicine so cutting-edge they could be scalpels. The SF Doctor will see you now.
Adam Roberts

A PRACTICAL GUIDE TO THE RESURRECTED

TWENTY-ONE SHORT STORIES
OF SCIENCE FICTION AND MEDICINE

edited by Gavin Miller and Anna McFarlane

Medicine is advancing at a breakneck pace. Genome editing, lab-grown organs and advanced bionics are all on the horizon - our lives are going to change dramatically. We'll live longer, be healthier, and become godlike. Or some of us will, anyway.

Through a series of short stories, this anthology looks at the medical frontier and our future. What happens to society when the dead can be brought back to life? When big pharmacutical companies create illnesses as well as cures? When a chip in your brain can take away depression for good? Will it make us better?

Available from
Shoreline of Infinity Publications
 www.shorelineofinfinity.com
198 pages
paperback, £10

Stories by

Seth Marlin
Krishan Coupland
Christine Procter
Michael F Russell
Marija Smits
Suzanne Hodsder
EA Fow
Matthew Castle
Hazel Compton
Peter McCune
Maija Haavisto
Okaimame Oyakh
Sam Meekings
Adam Roberts

and more...

## Afterlife

He drank through the hallucinations
that tried to entwine him
in their silky ribbons.
Flakes of the lost world fell around him
like carnivorous snow.

The beast had been willing to let him
ride it, asking only his heart in exchange.
It left blackened tracks on the stone.
Something about the lake of fire
seemed familiar.

Eye makeup was the only mandatory
attire, these days, and the more it looked
like the holes in a skull, the better.
Sometimes there were teeth—
Batesian mimicry.

The extra limbs were already
beginning to form.
He hoped they would end
in serrated claws—
for self-defense only, of course.

One deck of cards could predict futures;
the other reflected only the past.
But someone had shuffled
both decks together. They knew
where they were going, though.

It's better to be the monarch
of a dying planet
than not to be a king
at all. Everybody was falling
outward from its center, falling apart.

Green leaves against the black
of space. *That's* inspiration.
He was returning to the tools
of a simpler time: a manual typewriter,
hand-rolled cigarettes, pink nail polish.

With the right wardrobe, he wouldn't
need to speak. Or think. He could
be headless. His nose and ears
had always been an embarrassment.
Who needed hands, anyway.

She turned away from the sun
to smile back at him.
She didn't turn *into* anything.
She disappointed him
in ways he had forgotten.

He kept the stumps of his hands
over where his ears had been.
He had many companions by then,
imaginary and otherwise, some of whom
made him regret earlier decisions.

Some of whom regretted nothing.
Not even the sacrifices, the blood-
drenched furrows. He watched
an imaginative god rise
from a leveled horizon.

**F.J. Bergmann**

# Flagship

Our highly advanced society is administered
entirely by the Muses. We have five of them:
Barista, the Muse of caffeinated beverages;
Mielle, the Muse of apiculture; Cake, the Muse
of high-calorie pastry; Buttress, the Muse
of architecture; and Bazooka, the Muse of dissent.
The terrain of our world, no matter how precipitous,
is rigorously gridded, though considerable latitude
is allowed with respect to how each grid-square
populates itself (variety in temperature, elevation
and humility is encouraged). Bees form the bulk
of our citizenry. A minimum number of sunlit
days are mandatory, except in the prison squares.
Clouds form as a cooperative venture between
pastry and architecture – where did you think
they came from? Designated blimps tug
clouds into position, then Bazooka gives
the signal to let the bombardment begin.

*F.J. Bergmann*

F. J. **Bergmann** lives in Madison, Wisconsin, USA, edits poetry for
Mobiusmagazine.com, and imagines tragedies on or near exoplanets. Work in
*Abyss & Apex, Analog, Asimov's*, and elsewhere in the alphabet. *A Catalogue of the
Further Suns* won the 2017 Gold Line Press chapbook contest and 2018 SFPA
Elgin Award.

## Meganuera Monyi

Well, I ain't no chopper, baby.
Didn't come to mist your crops.
I just got the drop on this lamb.
Gonna drop 'im on those rocks.

Yeah, I'm gonna drop in for dinner,
get right at his innards. Gonna daub
my masticating mouth bits with his
soft little fleece suit. Little fleece suit.

Got here through a wormhole, babe.
Ain't May 2004 where I'm from, hon!
Sorry to cause so much trouble.
Sorry to bust your time/space bubble.

I'm just an eight-foot dragonfly.
Relax. Yer too skinny to scarf.
Don't do cotton burritos in bikinis,
even itsy bitsy teeny weeny polka-dotted ones.

Fifties caught up with you, babe.
Cold war fantasies of giant radioactive
ants had you freaked. I just decided
to visit, spin a few platters from the past.

Cop some fast food, cruise the valley
with my top down, so to speak.
Grab a sheep. Go on the lam
before heading back to my Cretaceous crib.

G-g-g giant d-d-dragonfly!
Don't go flub flub flub
when I'm in flyin'mode. Just hover, hon.
Suck back a few sanguine shakes.

Meganuera monyi, Cretacious cutie.
Gonna sock it to you, babe,
in psychedelic moiré colours,
all four wings ablaze!

Leda only had a Don Juan
gone-by-dawn swan, sweetheart –
a smooth talker, great lover maybe –
but he knocked you up, didn't he?

I may be more mechanical,
but I can dance on a dime,
hover, feint left or right
better than your best boxer.

Hey! I've got compound eyes.
I see you comin' and goin'.
Know all three of my right feet
from my left. Am totally tubular!

Fast shuffle, fox tot, waltz –
I got 'em covered. Flap flap.
Don't need a gat, pork pie,
zoot suit, or any flim flam scam.

Zzz Zzzz Zzz. C'mon, honey,
shake your money maker!
I'm the dude who can take you
to another era. Fly with me!

**Richard Stevenson**

*from Deep Wheel Orcadia: a future fantasy*

---

**Richard Stevenson** recently retired from a 30-year teaching gig at Lethbridge
College in southern Alberta. He has published thirty-one books, most recently
a long poem sequence on the Clifford Olson serial murder case, *Rock, Scissors,
Paper* (2016) and a collection of haikai poems and sequences, *A Gaggle of
Geese* (2017).

## Eynar an Olaf speir at the neow teknolochy

"But hoo's hid wirk?" asks Eynar, pooran
a beer. "A'm no sure," says Olaf,
"But yin arkaeolojist, ken, ach,
whit's her naem, telt hid lik this –"

The yoleman grebs twa empie glesses
an a pock o nuts an steers
this subtle injines trow the warp
o time, represented noo

by rings o spirit on the bar.
"The drive maks a pock, see,
o hyperspace tae win trow,
so's hid can exceed relatievistic

constraints." "Ya but," says Eynar, "A thowt
the haird limits wis more or jeust
teknolojiecal. Whit wey
can thay avoyd a catastrophic

temporal paradox, eh?" Olaf
taks a drowt o his ael an says,
"Ya weel. Best kens. An Best kens
thay maan, fer hid's bad enof tae loss

the last bit o the last bit
o wir shippeen ithoot messan wi yin
fuckan multieversal anomalies
an aa." An Eynar, no drinkan, says,

"A'll drink tae that", lukkan ower
the empie taebles an grayan hair,
an weyghan the wirth o his business, the cost
o his stock, the size o his saeveens, the price

o a ticket tae Ross or Alpha Centauri
an runnan the nummers again, an pooran
Olaf anither, an wipan awey
the trails o the hyperdrive fae the bar.

*Harry Josephine Giles*

# Eynar and Olaf Question the New Technology

"How does it work then?" asks Eynar, pouring Olaf his beer. "I'm not sure," says the yoleman, "But that archaeologist, oh, what's her name, told me it was like this."

Olaf grabs two empty glasses and a packetpocket of nuts and steers these subtle engines through the warp of time, represented now

by the rings of spirit on the bar. "The drive makes a pocketpacket, see, of hyperspace to travel through, so's it can exceed the relativistic

constraints." "Yes, but," says Eynar, "I thought the limits were more than just technological. How are they avoiding catastrophic

temporal paradox, eh?" Olaf takes a draught of his bitter and says, "Yes well. Gods know. And Gods know they must because it's bad enough to lose

the last bit of the last bit of our shipping without messing with those fucking multiversal anomalies as well." And Eynar, not drinkings, says,

"I'll drink to that," looking over the empty tables and greying hair, weighing of the worth of his business, the cost of his stock, the size of his savings, the price

of a ticket to Ross or Alpha Centauri, and running the numbers again, and pouring Olaf another, and wiping away the trails of the hyperdrive from the bar.

# Olaf hishan his bairn tae sleep

The week by wis the bairn stairtan
tae waak: a hairdly-human knitch
o need, but waakan. Whan Olaf cam haem
fae the lighteen, his awn faither wis greeman
an Olaf thowt, "Whit noo, Bud?"

Will the bairn tak tae the ducts,
smoo roon labs o a night, clim
as possessed o a tail, dore tae be taen
oot i the yoles, lairn the hodden
neuks o the staetions an naems o the patrens

o lights? Lik Olaf, his mither an hers,
the wey bairns wis syn Orcadia
wis biggit: ship fock, staetion
fock, fock at nivver kent grund.
Or will this een be sometheen neow?

Olaf likes history – hid's aa he enjoyed
at the skeul, laernan hoo ither fock wis,
fer he loved what he wis. An so he kens
the warld is expandan faister again,
an that neow ships bring neow relays,

bring better links tae Mars, muckle
channels tae sype Orcadia whill aa
that bides is histry: staetions gaen
tae bruckalaetion, black hulks.
An mebbe this bairn'll be the een

tae brak the next speed barrier?
Sick o haem, dreaman o cities
o Mars, dreaman o meanan more.
Or bide an love a dwynan piece?
An whit o this futurs is bruckit most?

*Harry Josephine Giles*

# Olaf lulling his child to sleep

Last week the child started to walk: a hardly-human bundletruss of need, but walking. When Olaf came home from the lighting, his own father was grinblubbering, and Olaf thought, "What now, FriendChildLove?"

Will the child enjoyexplore the ducts, slinksqueezenose into meat labs at night, climb as though he had a tail, demandpesterbabble to be taken out in the boats, learn the hiddendarklonelyobscure nooks of the stations and names of the patterns

of lights? As did Olaf, his mother, and hers, the way he guessimagines children have since Orcadia was built: ship people, station people, people who never knew groundearth. Or will this one be something new?

Olaf likes history. It was all he enjoyexplored at the school, learning how other people were, because he loved where he was. And so he knows that the world is expanding again, and that new ships bring new relays,

bring better links to Mars, bigsignificant channels to draindry Orcadia until all that livestayremains is history: stations gone to ruindestruction, black hulks. So maybe this child will be the one

who breaks the next speed barrier? Sick of home, dreaming of cities of Mars, of meaning more? Or stayliveremain and love a piningfadingwithering place? And which of these futures is the most broken?

**Harry Josephine Giles** is from Orkney and lives in Edinburgh. Their latest publication is *The Games from Out-Spoken Press*, shortlisted for the 2016 Edwin Morgan Poetry Award.
They are studying for a PhD at Stirling, co-direct the performance producer Anatomy, and have toured theatre across Europe and Leith.
www.harrygiles.org

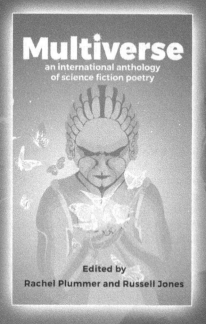

Lightning Source UK Ltd.
Milton Keynes UK
UKHW021055280519
343453UK00005B/129/P